A SUMMER OF INNOCENCE

When Harry Mitchell comes back into Jessica's life after an absence of nineteen years, she is disappointed to find that he appears to have no recollection of either her or the intimate relationship they had once shared. Perplexed as to whether he is now interested in her or her eighteen-year-old daughter, Jessica is determined to find out, once and for all, exactly what game Harry is playing. His answers are somewhat surprising!

Books by Jeanette Richards
in the Linford Romance Library:

IN LOVE'S IMAGE

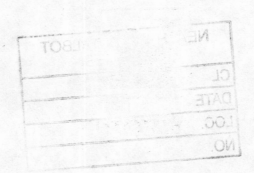

JEANETTE RICHARDS

A SUMMER OF INNOCENCE

Complete and Unabridged

LINFORD
Leicester

First published in Great Britain in 1994 by
Robert Hale Limited
London

First Linford Edition
published 1996
by arrangement with
Robert Hale Limited
London

British Library CIP Data

Richards, Jeanette
    A summer of innocence.—Large print ed.—
Linford romance library
    1. English fiction—20th century
    I. Title
    823.9′14 [F]

    ISBN 0–7089–7905–X

Published by
F. A. Thorpe (Publishing) Ltd.
Anstey, Leicestershire

Set by Words & Graphics Ltd.
Anstey, Leicestershire
Printed and bound in Great Britain by
T. J. Press (Padstow) Ltd., Padstow, Cornwall

This book is printed on acid-free paper

For my children, Susan, Cheryl, John and Colin. With very special love.

1

JESSICA HILTON hummed happily to herself as she strolled along the bustling Surrey high street. This was to be the start of a new beginning, she could feel it in her bones. The course she had followed at the local polytechnic, in word processing and office skills, had at least been successful in that it had given her enough confidence to apply for the job in the first place. Right now, it just seemed unbelievable to her that she had actually managed to get the position, especially since it had attracted over fifty applicants, most of whom had looked to her keen eye to have been at least ten years younger than her own somewhat ancient thirty-five.

Still, she thought smugly, they had chosen her and for her part she was just as determined to prove to them that they had made the right decision. Not that she had set her sights too high to begin with. After all, she had been away from the job market for more than eighteen years and believed that a small beginning was a way of getting your foot in the door.

She was only too thankful that the past was now over; that she was finally divorced, and could at least start looking to the future. With this in mind, the advertised position in the local *Gazette* for a receptionist, with no previous experience necessary, at Franklin and Sons, a small family firm of printers, had seemed the ideal place to start her journey along the road to recovery. She had decided that once established amongst the working class who knew what talents she might find she possessed?

Jessica gave herself credit for only a slight faltering of step when she reached the imposing double doors and saw Franklin & Sons, etched in large gold letters on the glass thereby heralding her arrival.

Taking a deep breath she pushed open the glass doors and walked through the entrance to what she hoped was to be the start of a better life.

"Hello," exclaimed a voice at her ear, as she glanced around uncertainly. "I'm Corinda Evans, Tony Franklin's secretary."

Jessica had already turned towards the speaker by this time and for some unknown reason she found she was relieved that the woman was about her own age. She returned the woman's smile with a thankful one of her own; it looked as though she would at least be shown the workings of the place and not be expected to know everything straight off.

"I was off sick when the interviews were conducted," Corinda continued to explain, "so I didn't have a chance to meet any of the applicants."

"Well, I'm pleased to meet you now," Jessica said impulsively, noting the other woman's eyes flicker over her in quick appraisal. At least she seemed to approve, she thought thankfully, wondering at this childish notion she still nursed that she had to be liked by everybody. Another result, no doubt, of rushing into a marriage of convenience at sixteen without a thought of the consequences of such a drastic step. "I hope I live up to everyone's expectations," she added, somewhat nervously.

"I shouldn't worry too much about that," Corinda said breezily, indicating Jessica should follow her through the first door to their right. Nevertheless Jessica was a little put out when Corinda added, "At least Frances had the sense to choose a more mature applicant this time, which is something to be said in your favour."

Jessica grimaced wryly. "It is?" She was beginning to feel more ancient by the minute.

Corinda nodded. "Most definitely. Mr Franklin and his nephew have managed to drive away three under-twenty-fives between them — and that's only in the last six months!"

"Goodness." She began to feel the familiar trepidation knotting her stomach. "How did all that come about?"

Corinda shrugged. "It was Mr Tony's hollering — all bark and no bite you understand; and his nephew's philandering — charming as he no doubt is at it. One way or another it was enough to send the girls scurrying for cover."

Jessica decided she was in no hurry to meet this blustering owner of Franklin's or, for that matter, his bluebeard nephew. Especially since one disgruntled shout or misguided pass and they were likely to discover she was just a child herself merely disguised as an adult.

"Mind you," Corinda continued, apparently failing to notice Jessica's dismay, "it is some consolation that the rest of us are a friendly bunch, having survived all onslaughts and earned the tag of long-standing employees. And the only favoured relative is our very own charmer whom I have already mentioned.

Jessica was once more aware of foreboding creeping up from her toes. Perhaps all of this had been a mistake after all. Maybe it hadn't been such a good idea to find herself a job now that Chellie had started police training and was living in at the centre. In fact, she was sure that at this minute she felt younger than her daughter and that Chellie would be having no such qualms about her own future.

It was a ridiculous situation to be in of course, but then she had spent years agonizing over her situation before deciding finally to part from her husband. Ten years of misery, regret, and the loss of her youth.

Not that she could wholly blame Laurie for the situation they had got themselves into. What had seemed like a good idea to a desperate sixteen year old, had proved to be a disaster after a brief honeymoon period. How either of them had managed to stick it out for ten long years was now beyond her; for her part, however, the thought of bringing up a child alone had seemed even more fearsome.

Once the decision had been made and they had made the break, Jessica had been surprised to discover that a life apart was infinitely better than one spent alone inside an empty marriage.

She had not, however, managed to escape completely unscathed. The scars the experience had left on her, had caused her to shy away from making any sort of commitment. There had, therefore, seemed little point in actually divorcing Laurie, so the separation had lasted for seven years; only culminating now in Laurie divorcing her because he had met somebody else.

She realized Corinda was speaking to her and forced her thoughts back to the present.

"Not everybody has arrived yet,"

Corinda was explaining. "Once they do, I'll take you along and introduce you to some of them. Now let me see if you have everything you want." She broke off to rummage through the deep wooden drawers, then straightened, apparently satisfied. "If you should find you're lacking any item of stationery, just give me a shout."

"I will," she agreed, her eyes straying to the switchboard with its imposing array of buttons and lights. I hope you're not going to give me any trouble, she warned it silently.

Corinda noted her bemused expression and smiled encouragingly. "I take it you have worked a board before?"

"Well, yes," she conceded, swallowing hard, "but it was rather a long time ago."

"Then you should have no worries about the techniques of that one," Corinda told her cheerfully. "Franklins is not a company to take easily to change. However many years you're referring to, this switchboard is sure to follow the same principles as the boards did then." Her eyes continued to look amused. "When Tony Franklin refers to his old-established firm you will know exactly what he means."

"I will?" Jessica continued to look doubtful, both at the switchboard and what Corinda was getting at.

"You will," the woman repeated. "It means that neither the staff nor their equipment gets updated from one year to the next." She made a sweeping gesture with her arm which was meant to take in the contents of the room. "You can't have failed to notice what delightful antiques you're taking over!"

Jessica had noted; far from putting her off however, the well-used furnishings only served to make her feel more comfortable. After all, hadn't she managed to let herself get left way behind the times?

It was some consolation though, to realize that even if she had made many wrong moves her decision to bring

Chellie back to this Ewell suburb seven years ago had been the right one. That Brenton was the ideal place to settle, being just a stone's throw away from the house where she had been brought up by her paternal grandparents, raised alongside her father's younger brother.

Even given that her grandparents were no longer alive and that Mickie had emigrated to Australia, the familiar streets and the house where they had lived were still there for her, full of the memories of those happier times.

"Well, Jessica? What do you think? Will you settle here with us, or have I put you off completely?"

"I agree, the place is sort of quaint," she told her. She didn't add that the thought of meeting the firm's intrepid partners was playing havoc with her nerves. She decided that a change of subject was needed to divert the attention away from herself. "What a lovely chair," she exclaimed, with genuine admiration. When she walked round the desk, however, and actually seated herself down on the cracked brown leather, its protesting creaks made her position feel none too safe. Goodness, she thought, I hope I'm not the one it lets down after all these years. Then her eyes were drawn once more to the switchboard, which from such close quarters appeared to have grown in stature. Still, she thought with some relief, Corinda was right, it didn't look too different to the one she had worked as a junior relief.

"I take it you were shown the word processor?" Corinda queries, tapping the top of the machine. "The reason I ask is because I can't always rely on matters being conducted properly when I'm away."

Jessica nodded happily; she was beginning to feel more confident by the minute. "It's not unlike the one I trained on and I was given a test at the interview." Her brow creased. "I was never actually told how I got on though."

"Not to worry about that," Corinda

said cheerfully. "You obviously impressed somebody or you wouldn't be here now."

For obvious reasons, reception was situated directly off the main entrance. As the staff were still arriving, this resulted in a steady stream of faces passing the door, many of whom stopped to bid them good morning.

After answering yet another greeting, Jessica turned to Corinda. "How many people actually work here?" she asked nervously. "I got the impression it was only a small company — or at least, the advertisement stated it was."

Corinda stared at her thoughtfully. "Probably the fact that it is an old-established family firm gives the wrong impression. I wouldn't say it's large, but besides those of us who work in the offices there are the men on the factory floor."

Jessica's eyes widened. "I didn't realize there was a factory on the premises."

"Didn't you?" Corinda gave her an

amused grin. "How did you think we printed the work? Sending everything out would be far too expensive; besides, no printer worth his salt farms all his work out."

"I suppose not," agreed Jessica, biting her lip. "I just hadn't given that side of it much thought." She sighed and leant back in her chair. "I think the trouble is I am so out of touch with the working world." She hesitated, studied Corinda's face, then made up her mind. "It has been rather a long time you see."

Corinda perched herself on the side of the desk, which caused her already short skirt to rise even further and expose far more stockinged leg than Jessica felt she possessed.

"You don't have to explain to me," she said gently, leaning across and patting Jessica's hand reassuringly. "And you are not to worry about it either. None of us here warrant losing any sleep over." She straightened and looked thoughtful. "I've been here ten years myself so the firm can't be that bad can it?"

Goodness, the same number of years as she had been married. Well, that didn't say much, for, hadn't she stuck it out for that long herself and she had been far from happy? She realized that Corinda had asked her a question. "I'm sorry, I didn't hear what you said."

She laughed. "You are getting yourself in a state aren't you? I just asked if you had been raising a family and that was why you hadn't worked for a while."

"Something like that," she mumbled, not wishing to unburden herself completely on her first day. Besides which she had always been one to keep her feelings to herself. She had learnt that much over the long, lonely years.

"I think the best thing to do would be to introduce you to Mr Franklin himself and maybe a few of the staff," Corinda exclaimed cheerfully, unhoisting herself from the desk and running her hands over trim hips. "Then you can see for yourself that there are no ogres amongst us."

Jessica followed the girl out of the room and along the corridor. As they walked, she noted the building was old and in need of redecoration, but in some ways she was glad of this because it made the company seem far less imposing. She took note of the number of closed doors they passed before Corinda stopped outside one, knocked sharply, then opened it and peered in.

"Mr Tony, I've brought our new receptionist along to meet you." She stepped aside and held the door open wide. "Tony Franklin meet Jessica Hilton."

"Come in, come in," demanded the gruff voice from the other side of an imposingly large desk. "I won't bite."

That's not what I've heard, thought Jessica, nervously taking a few steps forward.

"Come on, come on," he beckoned vigorously, whilst chewing on a cigar

15

stub. "I can't see you from there."

Corinda shut the door, took her arm and led her forward. "Don't let him bully you Jessica," she told her whilst fluttering her lashes furiously at the man. If you let him get away with it he'll make your life a misery."

Jessica was amazed. Did people really talk that way to their employers? Goodness, she had been in her own little world for far to long. "I'm very pleased to be working for you, Mr Franklin," she told the portly man, holding out her hand politely.

Tony Franklin grasped her hand firmly, then as he let go and she withdrew it, he picked up a pair of horn-rimmed spectacles, put them on then peered at her over the top of them.

That was a waste of time, Jessica thought, then jumped back as his voice boomed at her across the desk.

"You can call me Tony — Mr Tony, if it makes you happier." He leaned back in his chair, clasped his hands together as if he was about to pray, then leant his chin heavily on the fingertips. "You're not likely to burst into tears every time I speak, are you girl?"

Jessica knew she couldn't promise any such thing, but since he was waiting with raised brows for an answer, she felt bound to oblige. "I-I hope not," she managed finally.

"I hope not too," he muttered gruffly. "Can't stand snivelling women."

"If you hadn't bullied the other girls, then they would still be here now," Corinda told him firmly. Briskly she walked across to the desk and picked up a wad of papers. "As it is, Jessica is older and more experienced, so she is unlikely to put up with your whims."

Jessica peered at him anxiously, wondering how he was going to take Corinda's scolding, especially since much of it wasn't true and she was no more experienced than the youngsters he had previously chased away.

Tony threw back his head and

17

laughed heartily. "Well she doesn't look very old to me. I do note, however, that she is a pretty blonde; though not such a dumb one I take it?"

Jessica's eyes widened. Chellie was always telling her she looked young for her age and it was true that her hair was naturally fair. She would, however, never have been so presumptuous as to have described herself as a blonde and certainly not a pretty one. She suddenly warmed to this elderly, blustering man who was her new boss, and immediately the corners of her mouth went up and her eyes crinkled. "I hope you won't find me dumb Mr Franklin, er, Mr Tony, but I may need a little time to get used to things."

Tony's mouth fell open in pleased surprise, as the warmth flooded Jessica's face, lit up her eyes, and enhanced her looks still further. It was a long time since he had met anybody quite so unassuming, he thought admiringly.

"Well done Jessica, that's put him in his place." Corinda waggled the wad of papers under Tony's nose. "I'll type this lot up and let you have them back again to sign. Come on, Jessica, I'll show you where my office is on the way back, in case you should need to find me."

Jessica flashed Tony an apologetic smile before turning and following Corinda towards the door. Strange she thought, but for some reason she was beginning to feel rather sorry for him.

Corinda stretched forward to grasp the handle when the door was flung open and she was knocked sideways.

"Sorry Corinda," apologized the tall, broad-shouldered man, not looking a bit penitent. "I didn't realize you were there."

"Well you wouldn't unless you could see through wood," she said wryly, rubbing her sore shoulder ruefully. "Perhaps if you slowed down a bit you'd be less of a danger." She turned away from him, "This is Harry Mitchell, Jessica, the one I told you about." Her neat, pencilled brows jigged comically, and were still arched when she added, "He's Tony's nephew and our Production Director."

Jessica hadn't moved from the spot where she had been standing when the door burst open. She seemed unable to take in Corinda's frantic gestures that this was the man she had been warned about. Instead, she continued to stand wordlessly, staring at the man whose bulk seemed to fill the door-frame.

"Jessica!" Corinda peered at her worriedly. "Are you OK? You look kind of strange."

With a supreme effort Jessica managed to pull herself together, hold out her hand, and shake that of the man she never thought in all her wildest dreams she would ever see again. It had been nineteen years since she had looked on the face that had haunted both her sleeping and waking moments, and in all those years he had hardly changed at all. Whilst she . . . "Pleased to meet you Mr Mitchell." She tried to smile but her mouth wobbled dangerously.

How strange to hear that his name was really Harry, when she had only ever known him as . . .

"Mitch," he corrected cheerfully, smiling down at her and appearing not to notice her dilemma. "And you must be our new receptionist. I've already been along to introduce myself but, of course, you weren't there. Let's hope you last longer than the others, eh Corinda?" He put a friendly arm round the girl.

"Mind the shoulder," she yelped, pushing him off.

Jessica continued to stare up at him, hoping for some sign of recognition, but there was none. Had she really changed so much, she wondered? The years had been kind to him. It was only his attitude towards Corinda that disturbed her slightly, causing her to imagine that his friendly warmth was a little too strained. But then it could be that she was making far too much of Corinda's previous warning.

She had to bear in mind that it had

been a long time, that even then he had been a man, whilst she had been just a girl. Was it any wonder that he didn't recognize her, given that she had changed, grown into a woman, grown old before she had had a chance to be young?

After a few more exchanges Mitch vanished once more from the office. But no longer from her life, she thought with a shiver of trepidation. How was she going to cope now with the renewal of the acquaintance after so much water had passed under the bridge?

She followed Corinda back along the corridor on legs that seemed determined not to support her, barely acknowledging or even noticing where Corinda indicated her office was to be found. She could hardly believe that the man whom she had kept in her heart for all these years had once more turned up in the very place in which she had chosen to work.

If it had happened seven years ago, when she had first come back to the area, she would have understood it. For Mitch had been her main consideration in returning to the only place she knew he might be found. How strange it now seemed, to think that he had been so close all these years, yet so elusive.

She nodded absently when Corinda excused herself, saying she had to take some papers back to her office. When she had gone, Jessica walked round the wide, antique, mahogany desk and sank down in the swivel chair, thankful that she was hidden from passing eyes by the word processor.

Her head felt strange, as if it were unable to cope with the shock of seeing the only man who had filled her dreams since she had been a young girl. Yet he hadn't even recognized her! That much hurt, deeply.

That she had changed so much physically she didn't find hard to believe, for one did indeed grow a great deal from the age of sixteen to thirty-five. But the fact that they had become so close, been so intimate!

She shied away from using the word but it refused to be dismissed, and as her mind went back over how it had been, she tried to let the painful memories wash harmlessly over her.

She remembered the lonely childhood she had endured when her father's executive position had frequently taken him abroad; always accompanied by her mother who appeared totally oblivious of the fact that a mother's place was with her child.

It was true that she had been left in the care of her paternal grandparents, but she had still felt rejected; had always felt that she was in the way; had been convinced that she had not really been wanted. Was it any wonder that her emotional maturity had suffered? That she had been only too eager to grasp at the first gesture of affection shown to her? That her desperation to be loved and needed matched Mitch's willingness to oblige?

She felt her heart miss a beat, as she felt again the force of that first meeting.

She had been a mere thirteen years old, possessing all the painful emotions that such a tender age brought with it, and she had fallen for Mitch — hard.

She couldn't speak of these feelings to him, not then; he was her Uncle Mickie's friend and a manly nineteen.

But he had been kind and friendly, teasing her gently about her open admiration and saying it was a pity she wasn't a few years older.

How she had fiercely longed to grow; wished the years away until she was old enough for him to care. That time had come, three years later, when she was still only a child inside and he was a man who should have known better.

Yet how could she blame him? What man would have resisted when a girl was falling at his feet in adoration? Certainly not Mitch, whom she felt she had known all her life, and who was by now, showing he cared.

She remembered the pain and the joy of that first and only time of love. Remembered how he had assured her that it would be all right and how she had believed him. When she had realized, to her horror, that she was pregnant, it had been too late, Mitch had already vanished abroad on an assignment for his newspaper, and she was too inexperienced to know how to contact him to let him know.

Once more she had felt abandoned. Again, felt vividly the pain of an enraged grandmother's anger, only realizing later that it was anger brought on by a fear of her parents' reaction.

She had refused to name the father, had taken the only way out she knew. Laurie had been as much a victim as she herself had been when he agreed to marry her. He lived a few doors away from her grandparents' house and had admired her from afar, but he was only a few years older than she was, and just as lacking in experience.

The fact that she had spent some time in his company in the past, was enough to convince her grandmother that Laurie must be the father. When a hasty marriage was suggested, she was only too happy to agree.

Could she really have been so innocent as to believe that the marriage had any chance of working? Had she ever forgiven her parents for sending their permission so readily without question?

Jessica ran agitated fingers through her layered fair hair. Of course she had, in fact she had managed to forgive everyone except herself. She laid the blame squarely on her own shoulders for the disastrous years after Chellie had been born. Had realized it was inevitable when Laurie had been unable to accept Chellie as his own. They were children — what could she expect?

For her part she was determined that Chellie would not have the unhappy childhood she herself had had, which was why she had stuck with Laurie until they could stay together no more. Now Mitch was back in her life and he no longer knew her.

Jessica picked up a wad of papers from the desk and sifted through them unseeingly. Had she any right to disrupt her life that had been so hard fought for? Could she really hope to mean anything to Mitch after all this time?

No, she decided, taking a shuddering breath. She would try to avoid him as much as she could, and if that proved impossible, then she would look for a position elsewhere.

"Right, Jessica," exclaimed Corinda, walking back in to the office and bringing a welcome break from her thoughts. "I'm back to show you a bit more on the processor. We'll start off with these invoices and go on from there."

2

JESSICA wasn't sure whether to be thankful or sorry when her first day came to an end without Mitch putting in another appearance. Fresh doubts niggled away inside her head as she tidied her desk in readiness to leave.

She thought about the telephone calls he had received during the course of the day, all of which she had put through with a cursory, 'For you Mr Mitchell', thereby ignoring any insistence on his part that they be on first-name terms, the reason being that she could not bear to address him as Mitch. Could not in fact imagine being able to do so without giving herself away with her tone of voice. She was therefore doubly thankful that he had not shown up to rectify the misunderstanding — wasn't she?

Jessica buttoned up her coat, put the switchboard through to night service, then gave a last glance round the neat office, before opening the door and walking slowly along the short passage to the main entrance. There was already a steady stream of staff leaving the building, but a quick glance at the faces told her that Mitch was not amongst them. she had safely got through one day at least she thought thankfully, turning out of the building and making for the bus stop.

Jessica had been waiting in the queue for about ten minutes when the sleek silver car pulled up alongside. She glanced at it curiously not really thinking it had anything to do with her.

The window slid down and to her bemusement a familiar head appeared in the opening. "Can I give you a lift Jessica?" Mitch asked. "I have to pass your place to get to mine."

She was uncomfortably aware of the interest shown by the other occupants of the bus queue, and for this reason only, she nodded mechanically, opened the door and got in.

"That's it," he said pleasantly. "Do up the seat belt, we don't want anything to happen to you."

Jessica gave him a fleeting glance as she fumbled with the strap, which to her dismay appeared to be twisted.

"Let me," he urged, taking the strap from her hands, untwisting it and pulling it across her chest to anchor it in place.

Away, as she now was, from watchful eyes she was beginning to regain her composure. "How do you know where I live?" she asked, before she could stop herself. She kept her eyes firmly averted but was nevertheless conscious that his gaze was still on her.

"I looked it up on your application form," he said easily. "Let's just say I was curious."

Since he still wasn't admitting to having known her, she thought dismally, why then had he gone to the trouble of checking up on her? She glanced out of the window as Mitch turned left into her street. It wasn't far — she could have easily waited for the bus.

"I believe this is it," he said cheerfully, pulling up in front of the purpose built maisonette. "At least it saved you a long wait. The 59 is a notorious route."

"Thank you, Mr Mitchell," she muttered primly, completely ignoring his attempts to make conversation. Her natural instinct was to ask him in for coffee, but she ignored this as well, telling him firmly, "I'll see you in the morning."

The disappointment that flickered across the rugged features took her by surprise and she slammed the car door shut rather a little too hard. "I'm sorry, Mr Mitchell," she apologized. "It slipped out of my hand."

"Think nothing of it," he smiled warmly. "And, Jessica, can't you call me Mitch? It sounds so much less formal."

She felt her resolve slipping and gave him a tentative smile. "I'll try to remember," she agreed, but was still unable yet to put it in to practice.

She walked round to the side entrance without a backward glance, but as she put her key in the lock she was well aware that he was still sitting there, his eyes watchful. She let herself in and hurried up the stairs to the second floor, eager to watch him pull away. But when she peered through the netted windows she was disconcerted to find that he had already vanished into the night.

She sank down on to the sofa her whole body trembling with reaction. He was showing an interest in her, that much was obvious, but why? He had shown no recognition when they had met and had given her no indication since that he had any recollection of her at all. Why then had he offered her a lift and taken the trouble to find out where she was living?

She could find no answers to such

questions, she only knew that despite not having seen him for so many years she still felt exactly the same attraction for him as she always had, and that was dangerous.

She tried to dismiss him from her mind and bring her thoughts back to wondering how Chellie had fared at training school. But her mind refused to be stilled, and she remembered instead her daughter's reaction when she had told her the truth about her father, some three years after their separation. She wouldn't normally have taken such a step, but she felt that the girl deserved some sort of explanation as to why Laurie appeared not to care about her, and why he had never once asked to see her.

She could still see Chellie's face as if it was yesterday. The understanding dawning on the small expressive face that it was nothing that she had done that had turned her father against her, but was in fact something beyond her control. In fact, Chellie had thought the whole matter of her conception highly romantic; but then, thought Jessica with an inward smile, was she not her mother's daughter after all?

After the explanations were over their life had followed a steady routine, with only the occasional references from Chellie that maybe her father might turn up one day on the doorstep and whisk them both away in his arms.

Jessica had steadfastly ignored these wistful innuendos, unwilling to acknowledge that they were an echo of her own fierce longings. Now four years on it looked as though part of her wildest dreams had become reality and Mitch was once more back in her life.

Yes, she thought wryly, but without any fond memories of you whatsoever; and when a feeling which closely resembled physical pain shot through her, she acknowledged just how much the reality hurt.

The ringing of the telephone brought her quickly to her feet; but she hesitated before picking up the receiver. Perhaps he had also taken note of her phone number, she thought tentatively, then dismissed the idea as foolish. Why, he would hardly have reached home yet.

"Hello, Brenton 5439."

"Hello Mum, is that you?"

"Darling, of course it's me, who on earth do you think it is?"

"I wasn't sure, you took an awfully long time in answering."

"Sorry dear, I've only just this minute got in."

"I know, that's what I'm ringing about. How did you get on?"

Jessica bit her lip took a deep breath and tried to sound casual. "Quite well I think dear. Now, how was your day?" Jessica knew she wouldn't get away with that scant piece of information and heard at once the exasperated intake of breath on the other end of the line.

"Never mind about my day, Mum, and stop changing the subject." A childish giggle echoed down the line.

"Were there any dishy men there to take your fancy?"

"Really Chellie, that is quite enough." But she was a bit quick with her response, and Chellie, as bright as a button spotted it immediately.

"Ah, so there were. Come on, Mum, tell me what he was like?"

Jessica sighed inwardly. How she wished Chellie wouldn't be so insistent that she found herself a man friend. She was always telling her she was wasted on her own, refusing to understand that she preferred it that way. "I don't know what you're talking about, Chellie. I was extremely busy sorting out the last girl's work; she left in rather a hurry."

"Um, that sounds interesting."

"Not especially. I think you are letting your detective mind run away with you. Apparently the last few girls were a bit on the immature side and couldn't take the pressure. That is why they left."

"I bet they'll get a shock when they

hear you get a fit of the giggles, Mum. In fact I bet they didn't believe you weren't ten years younger than you said. You could easily get away with it if you denied my existence, or at least reduced my age by a few years."

"I have no wish to do that," said Jessica firmly. "I happen to be very proud of you. Now, when are you coming home to see me?"

"Not this weekend I'm afraid." She followed the words with a long drawn-out sigh. "We're going on a fitness hike. Can't say I'm looking forward to it but it's all part of the package."

"There's nothing of you now," she exclaimed, conjuring up a picture of her daughter's slim figure in her mind. "If you lose much more weight they won't be able to find a uniform to fit you. Are you sure you're eating properly?"

"I'm a big girl now, Mum," she said gently. "You must stop worrying. Ah-oh, the money has run out. I'll phone you later in the week."

"Yes, do. Bye, dear, and thank you for phoning."

"Bye, Mum."

Jessica waited until she heard the click at the other end of the line before she replaced the receiver. An overwhelming surge of loneliness flooded through her. It was taking much longer than she had expected to get used to Chellie living away from home. The past few months since she had gone had seemed to drag.

Having always been a solitary person because of her upbringing she didn't make friends easily. Chellie was always telling her she should get out more, that she would never meet anybody stuck here at home. "You have punished yourself enough, Mum," she had declared on more than one occasion. "Devoting yourself to my upbringing is not the only way to live. Look at me," she had demanded. "Haven't I turned out all right? Then now is the time to find yourself a man to take care of you."

Chellie had been right about one thing, she had grown into a very attractive, but most important of all, an extremely caring young woman. Jessica knew that she would make a wonderful police-woman and would serve the public well.

As for her declaration that she find herself a man, as yet that had not been her primary aim. She had simply not been interested. She had been far too worried about the effect another father figure might have had on Chellie, despite the girl's assurances to the contrary. Besides, she realized now that she had always been in love with Mitch. Had never ever stopped loving him despite what he had done.

Yes, young lady, declared the voice in her head, but what was it exactly he did do? And it was true, he had done nothing intentionally to hurt her. He had loved her too, she was sure of that, even if he had never actually said as much. He hadn't known of her predicament, how could he, when no sooner had she discovered it herself than she had married the boy up the road.

What would Chellie say now if she knew that after years of living in Mitch's old area fate had suddenly pushed him back into her life?

A shiver ran the whole length of her body at the thought of that much-loved face smiling down at her after all these years. She turned and reached shakily for the kettle. She couldn't tell Chellie yet, she decided firmly, it wouldn't be fair. She had to find out a few things about him first, whether he was married or committed to somebody else before she even thought about starting any sort of friendship. Besides which, it still hurt deeply to think that he didn't know who she was, that she had meant so little to him that he had no recognition of her at all.

The water spurted up into her face and she realized she had absently over-filled the kettle. She tipped half of it back out and tried to still her dizzy thoughts and concentrate. She didn't feel like eating after the shock of the day, and decided on soup as an easy alternative to having to make herself a proper meal, which she felt sure she wouldn't be able to eat. I'll find out tomorrow, she decided, I'll ask Corinda about the employees and make sure that she tells me everything she knows about Mitch. Having made a decision she suddenly realized she was quite hungry, and managed to follow the soup with cheese and biscuits, and an apple, before settling down in front of the television for the night.

* * *

Jessica arrived at Franklins the next morning half an hour earlier than she needed to. She had the uneasy feeling that Mitch might again pick her up from the bus stop, putting her in his debt and therefore at a disadvantage. She wanted to get to know him again on her terms and was thankful when a glance round the parking area in front of the building showed her he hadn't yet arrived.

She used the key she had been given the day before to let herself in to the building, then made her way along to the offices.

By the time the rest of the staff started to arrive, she had sorted out the desk drawers, moved things around, and had everything neat and tidy and in the order she wanted them.

"My, we have been busy," exclaimed Corinda, walking into reception then stopping short to admire the rearranged office. "You must have been here hours."

Jessica smiled. "Only half an hour or so. It was easier to get things done without the telephone constantly ringing.

"I know the feeling. When I've taken over the board some lunchtimes, expecting it to be quiet, it's driven me crazy. The public can be so impatient."

"I know," Jessica agreed, wondering how she could casually bring up the subject of Mitch. Then she had an idea. "When you have time, Corinda, I'd be grateful if you could let me know a bit about the rest of the staff, and the directors of course. You know the sort of things, how long they have been with the company etc etc. It will be nice to have an idea about the kind of people I'm working with."

"Of course I will, Jessica, I'm always game for a bit of gossip."

Jessica looked startled. "That wasn't quite what I meant," she began, but Corinda just laughed it off.

"I'm only teasing; we women are naturally inquisitive." She moved forward hesitantly. "I am right in thinking you're divorced aren't I?"

Jessica brushed absently at an imaginary strand of hair on her forehead, a nervous gesture she had acquired as a child and which lately she found herself doing more and more. "Well, yes, but I did point that out on

44

my original application form."

Corinda help up her hand. "Nothing to worry about I assure you. It's just that I couldn't quite remember when Mitch asked me about you yesterday."

Jessica's eyes widened in disbelief. "Mitch asked you about me?" she repeated, feeling thankful she was at last able to say his name out loud without trembling.

"Yes, he did," Corinda agreed frowning. "Just being nosy I guess; still I'd be careful of that one if I were you."

She cleared her throat and crossed her fingers. "Is Mitch married then?" she asked, and was concerned to find she still sounded rather breathless.

"No he isn't." Corinda stared at her curiously. "What is all this then? A mutual admiration society?"

"Of course not," she defended, her fingers fluttering nervously at her throat. "I was just curious that's all." She cleared her throat. "As he looks to be in his late thirties, and rather good looking, I was sure someone would have snapped him up by now."

Corinda gave a slight toss of her head, but continued to look disapproving. "There is no on-going relationship either, as far as I know. So if you fancy him, Jessica, the coast is clear."

"It's nothing like that," she defended indignantly, trying not to show the relief she felt at this latter disclosure.

"Just as well," Corinda declared, looking suddenly thoughtful. "He's been carrying a torch for someone for several years now. A few of the girls here, as I warned you, tried to break through the barrier. But it always ended the same way with them being hurt when he couldn't seem to relate."

Jessica's heart sank with this latest revelation, yet what did she expect? The man was a normal healthy male for heaven's sake, the idea that he had been waiting for her all these years was sheer fantasy, the sort of thing that only belonged in books. She took a shaky breath. "These girls who caught Mitch's eye? Do they still work here?"

"Goodness no. Most of them found it impossible after he had taken them out and wined and dined them." She hesitated before adding, "Maybe bedded them as well for all I know. It would have been a loss of face to have to work in the same place and be ignored."

"Would he have treated them like that? Ignored them I mean?"

Corinda shrugged. "Probably not. I've never known Mitch to be vindictive, but they left anyway."

"How did his uncle take this dallying with the staff?" she asked curiously. "He must have noticed, since he had to keep replacing them."

Corinda stretched lazily and shifted her bag more firmly on to her shoulder. "Mitch can be a devastatingly charming man, as you will no doubt find out if his interest in you yesterday is anything to go by. He is also very genuine and his congenial attitude is extended to most people he comes into contact with including his uncle. Talking of whom, I had better take him along the mail before the next delivery arrives."

Jessica felt heartened to find that Mitch had not changed from the days when she knew him. She was, however, still put out to find that he was so popular with other women, not that she had any intention of becoming another one of his conquests to be loved and left again.

"As a matter of fact," Corinda confided, turning back as she reached the door, "there is nothing Mr Tony would like more than to see him happily settled down with a nice wife and a couple of kids. He has made no secret recently of the fact that he would be happy to retire and leave everything in Mitch's hands. The trouble is Mitch is still so restless and all the while he behaves like that, Mr Tony will just stay on." She opened the door. "I must go now. I'll pop back later and tell you what you want to know about everybody. How does lunchtime suit you?"

"That will be fine," she agreed, not wishing to let Corinda know she had already told her everything she needed to know.

The door had barely closed behind Corinda before it was opened again. Thinking the girl had forgotten something, Jessica took a few seconds before glancing up; when she did so the smile froze on her lips when she saw it was Mitch who had walked through the door, closed it softly, and was now advancing towards her.

3

MITCH reached her desk, slid easily in to the chair beside her and stretched his long legs casually in front of him. "I'm glad to find you here," he told her; and although she was aware it was irrational she immediately felt irritated. Just where did he expect her to be?

"I'd like you to type a few letters for me. I don't know if Corinda pointed out that I don't have my own secretary." He smiled warmly. "Usually I find the receptionist is happy to oblige."

I bet she is, thought Jessica grimly, ignoring how attractive the smile made his features and wondering just how obliging her predecessors had been.

"How do you like working in our little company?" he continued, ignoring the fact she had not answered his question. "I hope you stay with us. It will be nice to have a settled member of staff; we've had so many young girls passing through our hands."

Just whose hands was he talking about, she pondered, remembering Corinda's references the day before to his past. "Look Mr Mitchell — "

"Mitch," he broke in smoothly. "It sounds so old-fashioned to call each other by second names."

She shrugged and in an effort to ignore her fast-beating heart her next words came out rather sharply. "Mr Mitchell? Mitch? What does it matter the answer will be the same. I haven't had time to find out if I like working here, there are far too many interruptions allowing me to do too little work." She immediately regretted the words when she saw the shadow mask his pleasant smile, and watched with growing dismay as he unwound himself from the chair and slowly got his feet.

"Then I won't be the one to delay

you," he told her with a touch of cynicism. "I'll bring the papers back later — that is if you're not too busy to type them!"

"Of course," she assured him, attempting to smile. But it didn't reach her eyes and by his quizzical stare she knew that he was well aware of her insincerity.

"Until later then," he said, glancing back over his shoulder. Then the door banged shut and he was gone.

She sank back on the chair and wished for the hundredth time that she could relax in his company, but she couldn't. The shock of seeing him again had been bad enough, but hearing all those stories about his past from Corinda had complicated the issue still more.

She accepted the problem lay with her; after all the man couldn't be expected to be celibate. Looking at it as logically as she could, it appeared to her that she hadn't really grown up from the girl she had been when she had first known him.

She somehow felt suspended in time, as if she was waiting for Mitch to wake her up from that long summer of innocence. To be so naive as to get herself pregnant was bad enough, but to marry a man she hardly knew just to give the child a father, had been sheer foolishness. In fact, the whole thing was a series of actions by someone with a complete lack of emotional maturity, and now she expected Mitch to come along and tell her everything was all right; that she had made all the right decisions when she knew damn well she hadn't.

It was all going wrong, she thought miserably. All those years when she had dreamed of this moment, longed for it, she hadn't expected it to be like this. But it could be better — she sat up in her chair and stared unseeingly through the window to the forecourt beyond — if she made more of an effort and tried to forget that he now had a past, that they had ever met and to treat it like a completely new relationship. The immediate lifting of her spirits was enough to convince her this new attitude was right; she would try and meet his attempts at friendship half-way.

A sudden picture of the other girls who had wept over him flashed in front of her eyes and she felt the sinking of her heart. What if he treated her the same? A second rejection? She pushed the idea sharply to the back of her mind — she couldn't even stand the thought of such an idea.

She kept her head down and worked hard at getting the backlog of work cleared up and was surprised when Corinda appeared and told her it was lunchtime. "You don't have to work quite so hard," she told her with a smile. "They are not slave drivers here." She sat down next to Jessica and opened up a packet of sandwiches. "Have you brought something with you to eat?"

"Yes, I've got some crackers and an

apple," she replied, reaching behind her for her bag. "Though I must admit I'm not very hungry."

"Not on a diet are you?" She frowned, taking a large bite out of a cheese sandwich. "There is nothing of you now."

Jessica smiled and shook her head. "You sound just like my daughter Chellie. She's always going on about how little I eat and yet I stay at the same weight, have done since I was sixteen — " She broke off abruptly, having no wish to ponder on the fact that she was exactly the same size as she had been when Mitch had known her and still there had been no recognition. She realized Corinda was speaking to her. "I'm sorry, I didn't catch what you said."

"You are a dreamer, Jessica, aren't you? Is there anything worrying you? If the work is a problem I can go over things again."

She grinned wryly. "It isn't exactly the work that bothers me."

"Then it's your daughter. I noticed you mentioned her, does she work round here?"

"No, she's at the Police Training School, in Hendon." A wistful expression came over her face. "Chellie's extremely independent, not at all like I was as a child — though of course she is no longer a child," she corrected. "These days, at eighteen, they are at one with the world."

"I agree," nodded Corinda, taking another bite of the sandwich and depositing the wrapper in the bin. "My own daughter is much younger, only ten, but she is forever letting me know I'm way behind the times."

"You're married?"

"Divorced." She pulled a face. "Another statistic, like you I'm afraid. Not that I'm bothered, I'm living with a nice boy, Jack, have been for the past four years." She stared at Jessica. "Have you got anybody special?"

Jessica hesitated slightly before telling her, "Nobody at the moment." She was quite amused by the sympathetic look the other girl gave her, almost she thought, as though she had said she only had one arm. "What was it you were saying about Mr Tony?"

"He hasn't been feeling too well today, flu I think. He's asked Mitch to take over for him this afternoon so he can go home."

The mere mention of Mitch's name was enough to send the colour flaming in her cheeks. Thankfully Corinda appeared not to notice. "Who do you prefer to work for?"

"I don't mind either of them," she said airily, with a flick of her wrist. "Mostly I run the office by myself when they are here." She paused, frowning slightly. "Mitch is inclined to be a bit bossy when he first takes over, though it's more a clash of wills than anything else." She brightened. "Once he realizes I don't need him to tell me what to do he settles down." She glanced at her watch and got quickly to her feet. "Talking of which, I had better get along there and sort him out. We'll have to have our little talk about the staff another time."

Jessica watched her go then settled back to her work. The afternoon passed as quickly as the morning, and before she had realized the time it was five o'clock.

She tidied her desk, put on her coat and switched the board through to night service. With a final glance around the office she prepared to leave, and was just about to walk to the door when it opened and Mitch stood framed in the doorway. She blinked rapidly, trying desperately not to let him see the effect he had on her.

"Ah good, I've caught you. I had meant to get along sooner but I got caught up in business matters."

"Did you want me to get you a call? I can easily switch the board back through."

He waved his hand dismissively and stepped further in to the room. "Nothing like that, I wanted to offer you a lift home." He grinned boyishly. "I thought it better if I asked you here, keep picking you up at the bus stop might get both of us a bad name."

Oh Mitch, her heart cried out, if only you knew the truth of such a statement. How all my life I have tried to rectify my one mistake. She looked away from him, unable to deny him when he was regarding her in a way she didn't understand. "I've got some shopping to do," she lied. "It would be pointless you waiting." She was unaware he had moved to stand beside her until she felt his breath fan her cheeks.

"Why don't you like me?" he asked softly, while her body thrilled to his nearness. "Have I said something to upset you?"

She tried to compose herself, not let him see exactly what he was doing to her, "N-no, of course not, it's just that — " she tailed off lamely, then made the mistake of glancing up at him and found herself staring hypnotically into the familiar cobalt eyes.

They had mesmerized her when she was sixteen and they were doing exactly the same to her now. Would her foolish heart never grow up? Couldn't she see that she had never had the same effect on him, that he was unlikely to remember her if he hadn't done so up until now? Why did women leave their hearts in such unsuitable places? Why not do what you had decided, prompted the voice in her head, start off on a fresh footing as if you were just new friends. "I accept your offer," she told him, attempting to look grateful in the face of a wildly beating heart. "I can easily shop tomorrow, it wasn't anything important."

"We can always stop and pick something up on the way," he pointed out, keeping his eyes firmly on her face. "It won't be any bother."

She turned away so he wouldn't see she was flustered. "No honestly, I don't need the extras until my daughter gets home and that is unlikely to be before the weekend." She wondered if he could see she was lying. Damn Chellie phoning yesterday and saying she wasn't coming this weekend, at least if she hadn't made the phone call she might have sounded more convincing.

Thankfully he appeared not to notice and when she looked back he had turned away and was making his way to the door. She grabbed hold of her handbag and the magazine she had brought to read in the lunch-break, and followed him out of the room along the corridor and out through the glass doors to the forecourt beyond. She was acutely conscious of the curious glances they attracted from the other members of staff, most of whom were unfamiliar to her. I'll have to get Corinda to take me around the factory so that I can meet them, she thought, as they reached Mitch's car and he unlocked the door. At least then I won't be judged on my actions alone; after all I know I'm not the first girl he has taken home and they must all be thinking the same.

Jessica was surprised to find herself relaxing in his company once they were out of sight of Franklins and, as they cruised along in comfortable silence, she began to toy with the idea of asking him in for coffee.

"You mentioned a daughter," Mitch said suddenly, taking her by surprise. "Is she on holiday or staying with a friend?"

Jessica swallowed hard. "No, she's a police trainee. She's living in at Hendon." How strange it seemed to be telling him about his own flesh and blood. "She's still a baby really, barely eighteen. Though she wouldn't thank me for saying as much, she's fiercely independent."

The glance Mitch gave her lasted for several seconds before he looked back once more to the road, and for some reason she felt as if his eyes had pierced her soul. "Have you got any children?" she asked, in an attempt to change the subject, then she wished she hadn't when he gave his cynical reply.

"Not that I know of," he told her, turning left into her street. "But I'm sure if I had fathered a child I would have known about it, don't you?" He pulled up outside her house and turned off the engine. "Besides which, no natural woman could possibly keep that sort of thing from a man."

So her actions had termed her unnatural in his eyes, she reasoned, doing her best to ignore his raised eyebrows and questioning gaze.

"You're a woman, you tell me what you think?"

"I have no opinions on the matter," she told him firmly, as she struggled to unfasten her seatbelt.

His features softened and he leant forward. "Here let me help. These belts are a bit awkward."

The pressure of the belt across her chest was almost too much to bear, merely because she was aware his fingers were on the buckle. Such foolishness was making the whole situation get out of hand. She made up her mind not to ask him in after all, climbed out of the car as soon as he had released her, and slammed the door firmly behind her.

"Thank you for the lift," she said, as coolly as she could manage with her body on fire. "I'll see you in the morning." Then she walked up the path, fumbled in her bag for the keys then unlocked the front door, without once looking back.

Jessica closed the door behind her and leant fretfully against it. A few minutes later she heard the sound of the engine as Mitch drove away. He would never know what supreme effort of will it had taken not to open the door and rush back out there, she thought listlessly, as she climbed the stairs to her first-floor maisonette. During all the times she had thought of him over the years, she had never once dreamed that her body would react in exactly the same way as it had done all those years before. It was almost as if emotionally she had never matured; that somehow she had got caught in a moment of time where she had remained suspended.

She knew now that Laurie's taunts that she was frigid had not been true, and that what she was now experiencing was the slow awakening of long dormant sexual desire. She had a sudden longing for Mitch to take her back to the Downs where they had made love for the first and only time; to lay her down on the grass and make love to her now that she was a woman, the way he had when she was a girl.

She put her hands to her flushed cheeks, as a vivid picture of herself and Mitch lying in the long grass fulfilling their passion for each other flooded her mind. She hadn't brought out this memory for examination for many years. In the beginning it had been a regular occurrence, the one way she was able to get away from the humdrum existence she had unwittingly put herself into. Now, as she remembered the abandonment and impetuous desire that youth brought with it, she had a sudden craving for a return to those times and how it had been.

She loved Mitch still after all these years. She had always believed that the feelings she carried for him were simply memories of a time when she had been free from the shackles of an empty marriage. Yet she should have known that the emptiness she still felt when she had left Laurie was not the normal loneliness of being alone. It was an aching longing she had carried around with her for years to be with the one whose child she had carried.

She filled the kettle and switched it on as she tried to decide what was the best thing to do. There wasn't only herself to consider, there was Chellie as well. The girl had inherited her own romantic nature and expected her father to turn up and accept them both as if there had been no years between.

From what Corinda had told her that was unlikely to be possible. He had never married, she had said, because he carried a torch for a past love. That gave him a past that neither of them shared and, for all she knew, he could feel unable to love another while this unknown girl was in his heart.

There was also the fact that he might not be able to forgive her for not telling him about Chellie. What was it he had said in the car, that no normal woman would keep that sort of thing from a man?

She cracked eggs into a basin, added milk and cheese and buttered bread with barely a thought to what she was doing. How could he blame her for not telling him about the child when he was no longer around? How could he have let her face the music alone when she had been only a child herself?

She poured the mixture in to a buttered pan then poured tea into a china mug. No, there was no blame attached to either of their actions. She had done what she had thought best. She had used that same impetuousness that had got her into the situation in the first place to grasp at a way out of it.

The omelette was ladled from the pan, put on a plate and carried over to the table. But she found she couldn't eat it, and all she did was cut it up into small pieces and push it around her plate, until, exasperated with herself, she pushed it away, got up, and poured herself another mug of tea.

There had to be some way out of the situation, she thought dismally, rewarding herself with an extra spoonful of sugar to cheer herself up. She realized now that she could not leave Franklins and let him disappear from her life again, this time maybe for ever.

No, she mused, taking a mouthful of tea then coughing when it went down the wrong way, she wanted to get to know him again, see if it was possible to recapture the times as they had been, and make up for the years they had lost and which should have been spent together.

But he doesn't even remember you, echoed the remorseless voice in her head. How can you recapture something that might never have existed outside of your own wild imagination?

But he did care, her heart protested wildly. It had been no frenzied infatuation that had driven her into his arms; there had been no lustful obsession on her part to lose her virginity or on his part to take it.

She had grown up alongside him from the start of her teenage years until she was on the brink of womanhood. It was easy now to look back and realize what a girl she had really been, but that realization only came with the loss of youth and the gaining of experience.

Experience, she echoed. Was she any the more experienced now than she had been then? She would have to say no. The half a dozen times that she had fulfilled her obligations with her husband had been just that

— those of a dutiful wife. She had never managed to recapture anything of the ardent feelings or desires that she had experienced in Mitch's arms.

She had read in books that the first time was rarely the treasured experience one expected it to be. For her that had not been true. It had definitely been the only fulfilling moment in her life and everything she had fondly imagined and wanted it to be. It had been the aftermath that had caused her all the pain, and which was still causing her pain all these years since. Now she had a chance to put things right, to grasp at the opportunity of a few years of happiness, at least. Was she going to let it slip away?

4

JESSICA arrived outside the entrance of Franklins the next morning feeling emotionally drained and ragged. She had spent a night of restless tossing and turning and had only managed to get a few hours sleep before it was time to get up.

All her decisions from the night before now seemed grey and doubtful in the cold light of day, and she was once more uncertain of the future and what it might hold.

As she pushed open the door and walked along the passage, she knew now that in no way could she do as she had intended and treat Mitch casually as if they had never met. She already felt tense and strained and was aware that her attitude towards him was likely to be the same.

She opened the door of reception

and walked in, only to stop in her tracks when she saw Mitch was already there, perched in her chair idly tapping a ruler on the desk. She watched the welcome smile die on his lips when she was just too late to hide her accusing glare, and once more she cursed her expressive face. Mitch had often told her in the past, that with her eyes and face, she had no need for words at all.

"Jessica," he exclaimed, jumping to his feet and walking forwards to greet her. "I'm glad you're early. A few problems have come up and I need your help."

She was taken aback. He needed her help, but how could he when she was sure there were far more experienced staff only too willing to assist him? Her eyes narrowed as she struggled to hide the suspicion she felt.

"What help do you need exactly?" she asked, with a slight raise of an eyebrow. "I would have thought Corinda would have been the one to seek out, not me."

"That's exactly it," he answered, seemingly not a bit put out by her hostility towards him. "She phoned in sick about ten minutes ago, thinks she's caught the dratted flu off Tony."

"Oh, I see," she muttered, wondering exactly how she was going to be asked to help. "I take it that Mr Tony is not likely to be in either?"

"Not for a few weeks at least," he said grimly. "He suffers with his chest; something like this always lays him low."

He took hold of her arm and sat her down before perching himself on the desk in front of her. "I don't know how long Corinda is going to be out, which means we are going to have to get a temp in."

"And that's what you want me to do?" she asked, brightening considerably. "Ring the agency for a replacement?" Her face fell when he immediately dismissed the idea with a wave of his long, tanned fingers.

"Not yet I don't. I can't stand having strange girls in and out of my office — "

"Yet you don't seem to mind me," she challenged. "I'm in and out of Mr Tony's office all day and will be even more if Corinda isn't in." She waited to see if he would deny she was a stranger; realized that deep in her heart she was urging him to acknowledge her previous existence in his life. She stared into his face, carefully avoiding meeting his eyes, but his expression didn't falter, and when she did at last raise her own eyes to meet his gaze she found to her chagrin that his blue eyes held a hint of amusement.

She felt a surge of annoyance wash through her; just what game did he think he was playing? "How exactly do you intend dealing with the situation?" she asked, her tone more terse than she had intended. "I can't possibly be expected to do all the work on my own."

"I don't intend that you should,"

he told her, patting her hand as if to silence her protests.

Jessica snatched her hand away as his touch sent a wave of sensations crashing through her body. "Then what exactly do you intend?" she asked of him, whilst her head cried out in bewilderment that she had even dared to demand an explanation.

"I want to know if you'd be willing to stand in for Corinda until she gets back," he urged, seemingly not put out by her attitude. "I can then get a temporary to replace you."

She sank back on the chair and stared at him eyes wide. The idea had completely taken the wind out of her sails and knocked all her arguments for six. If she was in Tony's office working with Mitch they would be together all day. How would she be able to put up with that? An answering feeling of warmth began to creep through her body. It started at her toes and by the time it had reached her cheeks she had already given Mitch her answer. "It looks as if I don't have a lot of choice," she told him, shrugging her shoulders resignedly. "After all, you're the one in charge." But she realized by the look he was giving her, and which made her cheeks glow even redder, that he was beginning to doubt that he really was.

"Right then," he told her, getting abruptly to his feet. "If you ring Marker's Agency, their number should be on the index, you can make all the necessary arrangements.

"Will we need somebody today?" She looked tentative as she added, "It might be short notice." Though the only short notice she was really bothered about was her own, since it gave her hardly any time at all to get used to the idea of being in such close proximity to the man.

"The agency is used to such things happening. Most of their girls are on call in case of just such an eventuality."

She ran nervous fingers through her short curls as she watched him walk towards the door then he turned and caught her unguarded expression.

"Don't look so worried," he said softly. "I won't bite, I promise."

Then he was gone and she was left to arrange things with Marker's; which she did within ten minutes because she suddenly had a great longing to be in Tony's office working alongside Mitch.

It came to her in a rush: he was fast becoming such a part of her life that the minute he was out of her sight, a feeling of such loneliness and isolation swept over her that she found it hard to bear. This realization frightened her greatly, because only a few days ago she had accepted the isolation as being perfectly normal and she had been able to cope. Now that she knew there was something much more to life, realized that this all-encompassing feeling of needing and wanting to be needed was such an exhilarating heady experience, she was fast becoming addicted.

This was not a sensible way to feel at all, she thought with some dismay.

It meant that she no longer had any control over her life.

* * *

The next two days passed with heady speed for Jessica. She worked happily alongside Mitch, answering queries from customers and watching the way he expertly handled the men from the shop floor below. It also gave her a chance to become acquainted with them all, something that she had so far not managed, being shut away in the reception area.

She sat watching Mitch's bent head for a few minutes and found herself wishing that Corinda would stay away for a while longer, though she didn't really want her to be at death's door, just a bit too infirm to feel ready to come back.

She glanced at her watch and saw that it was nearly 2.30. Another few hours and her first week at Franklins would be over. How strange that it was only one week, when she felt as if she had worked here for ever.

"Are you anxious for the day to end?"

Mitch had noted her set expression, seen her look at her watch, and now he was watching her with that familiar unfathomable expression which she didn't know how to handle.

"Not at all," she said with honesty. "I'm surprised the time has gone so quickly."

"Are you Jessica?" he persisted, putting down his pen and swivelling his chair so he was directly facing her. "Have you enjoyed doing the work in there or would you prefer to be back in reception?"

He knew the answer perfectly well, she thought crossly, hadn't she told him so yesterday in so many words? Was he now persisting with the conversation to make her admit something she wasn't sure of or did he genuinely need reassurance? She stared at him thoughtfully, without meeting his eyes.

No, she couldn't imagine Mitch needing any assurance; he was much too self-assured.

"As I said before, Mitch, I find the work in this office much more interesting and lively." His expression didn't falter but his eyes flickered across her face willing her to meet his gaze. He was strong and she was fascinated to find that once again she could not resist his urging. As if in a dream she watched him get up from the chair and keeping his eyes fixed firmly on her own he came towards her. When he reached her side he leant forward and placed his hands one on each arm of her chair.

For a crazy moment she thought he was going to kiss her and she braced herself in readiness. But the moment never happened and, as he spoke, and she felt the disappointment flooding through her, she chided herself for such foolishness. For how could she work easily with the man if there was anything between them?

"I have a proposition to put to you, Jessica."

She stared at his face trying to imagine what such a proposition would entail and knowing in her heart that whatever it was she would agree. She sat back in the chair, trying to lengthen the distance between her face and his so that she could think more clearly. "That sounds ominous." She followed her words with a smile in an effort to diffuse the situation, frantically aware of the chemistry that was tangibly building between them.

Mitch's expression didn't alter, but the eyes below the thick bushy brows darkened from blue to navy. "How would you like to move out from reception and work with me instead?"

For a few seconds Jessica was shocked in to silence. She stared at him suspiciously to see if he was joking but his expression showed he was deadly serious. Her heart began to bang wildly. For this week to continue on after the weekend was more than she could have hoped for. She would be able to get to know him again, really get to know him over the weeks and months if she was actually working with him. Then her excitement died. "What about Corinda?" she asked, trying not to show her disappointment. "I can't possibly take over her job just because she has gone sick."

"There will be no question of it," he told her and her heart once more lifted. "My uncle is not in good health as you no doubt realize."

At this point Mitch moved away from her side, turned and stood with his back to her staring out of the window. She was thankful in one way because as he continued to explain the situation it gave her time to think more clearly. Since every thought showed itself clearly on her face it was better if he was not watching her every expression.

"He has long been anxious for me to take over the business here at

Franklins. The trouble is he thinks I'm irresponsible just because I haven't married."

Jessica unconsciously held her breath, then the noticeable silence was followed by a hollow laugh before his next words shattered her dreams.

"I've told him often enough that marriage, unless it was to the right woman, would never interest me." He spun round suddenly and stood staring at her with his hands behind his back, his eyes challenging.

So it is true, she thought with a sinking heart, he is still carrying a torch for another woman. Well, she thought with a defiant jerk of her chin, if he thought she was about to be another notch on his belt he was mistaken. After all these years she wanted more of him than that. And she met his gaze unflinchingly offering him a challenge of her own. "What exactly has your marital status to do with my working for you?" she asked coolly. "I don't mind what work I do as long as

I'm reasonably paid and treated with respect."

She regretted the words instantly when he looked as if he had been slapped. Then his face hardened and he was once more in control.

"If money is what bothers you then you have no need to worry. The job will be adequately paid." He shoved his hands in the pockets of his pin-striped trousers and began pacing the floor, while Jessica was forced to look on with growing sorrow at his obvious agitation.

"Tony is going to start coming in for only three days a week, but there will be plenty of work for Corinda to do on the other two days." He paused in his pacing to ruffle the dark hair at the back of his neck and a lump rose in her throat at the remembered boyish gesture from many years back.

He turned back to face her across the desk. "There's an office along the corridor that's only used for storage. I'm going to get it sorted out this weekend so that it will be ready for occupation on Monday morning."

"So the change-over is to be as quick as that?" She frowned. "What about a girl for reception; the telephones have to be answered?"

"That has all been taken care of. We are to keep the girl from the agency while they find us somebody more permanent."

So he had already arranged everything before he had approached her. He must have been sure of her answer or did he really care who worked for him as long as he was able to gain control of the business? She stared at him suspiciously. "Just exactly what work will we be doing if there is enough of Tony's work left for Corinda to do?"

"I shall be away from the office for some of the day, calling on clients and keeping them happy; you will be sorting out the follow-up correspondence."

She felt slightly deflated to find that he was not to be with her all day and acknowledged that, however much she might tell herself that she was free of him, it just wasn't so. "Is that what Mr Tony used to do, call on the clients?"

"Yes, but the courtesy part of the business has gradually deteriorated, mainly because of Tony's continuing poor health and his inability to get about as much. I intend to build it back up and make the company strong again."

So that it is financially healthy for you to take over no doubt, she thought grimly, then reprimanded herself for having such uncharitable thoughts.

"I'll still be acting as Production Director," he continued. "We can't afford to take on too many more staff. I'll just try to fit things in during the course of the day." He frowned at her. "That's where your expertise will come in to force."

"It will?" she managed, wondering exactly what qualifications he had in mind.

"Yes indeed. You can pacify the men and sort out their problems until I get back. Be a sort of PA if you like."

"I don't think I'll be much good," she giggled, suddenly seeing the funny side of things. "I hardly know the workings of a GTO machine or indeed of the small KORD. I'm sure the machine minders will find that out in no time."

Mitch smiled and immediately looked more relaxed. "You know that's not the sort of thing I mean. Tom Roberts, my Works Manager, will take care of the mechanical side of things. It's more their personal problems I want you to handle; soothe over any disputes until I get back." He stood smiling down at her, hands in pockets, feet astride. "So what do you say Jessica? Are you willing to give it a try?"

She swallowed the lump in her throat before attempting to answer. Didn't he realize that she would give anything a try that meant she would be by his side. She nodded, and said softly, "Yes Mitch, I'll give it a try." And his answering smile was so grateful it made her want to cry.

★ ★ ★

Jessica spent Saturday and Sunday cleaning and polishing the maisonette, in an attempt to take her mind off the subject of Mitch. She told herself the effort would not be wasted, despite the fact that Chellie was not coming home until next weekend, because it just might so happen that she would have company. That Mitch might take it in to his head to call round to discuss something with her, given the fact that he was only a few streets away, working in Franklins on the office they were both to share.

She sighed, the whole thing was unlikely, of course; he was probably far too busy to even give her a second thought. Much more likely to be working out just how much he would be worth in terms of hard cash when he took over the full running of the business.

She reprimanded herself for thinking such things, when she knew in her heart that Mitch had never been mercenary. Even given that she had adored him, and that her head had been so far up in the clouds that in her eyes he could do no wrong.

Why not ring him up, she thought with sudden daring, ask him over for a spot of lunch, or maybe even supper on his way home? No, not supper, she thought, with a dismissive shake of her head. That sounded far too intimate, it would be best not to get things on too friendly a footing, not if they had to work together.

But lunch wouldn't hurt, she pondered; she could easily make the excuse of finding out how he was getting on with the renovations, after all it was to be her office as well.

She made up her mind, walked into the hallway and picked up the telephone. It rang for a long time after she had dialled the number, and just when she thought that perhaps Mitch had only worked for a few hours, and was about to give up, she heard a click and then his familiar husky tones on the other end.

Her heart beat faster and she was almost unable to answer, wondering if the whole thing was a mistake.

"Hello, is anybody there?"

He sounded impatient now and Jessica could imagine his perplexed expression as she spoke to him. "It's me, Mitch, Jessica."

"Jessica, what a nice surprise, what can I do for you?"

She swallowed hard, let's hope he doesn't misconstrue the whole idea, she thought, as she asked him, "I thought you might like to call in for a bite of lunch. It won't be anything fancy mind, but I was preparing my own and I thought . . . " Her voice tailed off lamely and immediately Mitch's reply echoed down the line, the pleasure in his tone obvious.

"I'd be delighted to eat with you, Jessica. I was wondering whether to pop out and get a hamburger but the thought of a solitary meal amongst the debris of this office put me off." His words were followed by a silence and just when Jessica wondered if he was waiting for her to speak, and what she should say, his voice came back along the line.

"What time would you say suited you, Jess?"

She froze on the other end of the line at the use of the shortened version of her name. Her family had insisted her name was Jessica and apart from friends at school he was the only person who had ever called her Jess.

"Hello, Jessica, are you still there?"

It had obviously been a slip of the tongue, she decided, as she managed to gather her thoughts and give him a time. But as she replaced the receiver and walked back into the lounge she still felt a sense of confusion pervading her peace of mind.

She pushed her inclement thoughts to the background and concentrated on making the pastry for the steak and mushroom pie. It was one of Chellie's favourite meals and she hoped it would also go down well with Mitch. She peeled potatoes, chopped up spinach and carrots and had just got everything simmering on the stove and in the oven, when there was a ring on the doorbell.

"Whoever can that be," she muttered, untying her apron and running her hand hastily through her tousled curls. "Surely not Mitch, not this early." Through the glass-fronted door she could see the outline of two figures. Probably Jehovah's Witnesses she thought, just when I'm at my busiest. Then she opened the door and her eyes widened in dismay.

5

"WHY Chellie," her voice echoed her discomfort. "Whatever are you doing here?"

"That's nice, Mum," she chuckled, not a bit put out. "I come all this way to see you and this is the welcome I get." She turned to her companion, who had stood silently watching. "I told you I was an unwanted child, Scott, now you have the proof. Can we come in, Mum, it's chilly out here?"

A pang shot through her at Chellie's unfortunate choice of words. But it brought her back to the present and she ushered them both in through the door and up the stairs, exclaiming at her lack of manners. "I'm sorry darling, it's just that you didn't telephone to say there was a change of plans and I've sort of made other arrangements for this afternoon."

"What sort of arrangements?" But Chellie didn't wait for a reply, and thinking of her stomach as usual, she walked straight into the kitchen, stopped and sniffed appreciatively. "Yummy," she exclaimed. "My favourite pie unless I'm much mistaken." She turned and put her arms round her mother. "I'm glad to see you look after yourself now I'm not here. Do you think you can manage to stretch the meal to three?"

Goodness, she thought with some dismay, she had managed to get herself in to a sticky situation this time. She turned to answer her daughter and her eyes came to rest on the tall gangling youth hovering uncomfortably in the doorway. She suddenly felt very sorry for him. Really, Chellie was the limit. "I'm Jessica," she smiled, walking towards him, hand extended. "And as I understand it you are Scott?"

He looked relieved and shook her hand warmly. "I'm sorry for the intrusion Mrs Hilton."

"Jessica," she corrected.

He nodded. "Jessica. I told Chellie we ought to have rung you first."

"Nonsense," the girl said airily, "she is always pleased to see her only little girl, aren't you, Mum . . . " Her words tailed off as her gaze fixed interestedly on the table set for two. "So, those are your other plans. You're having somebody round for dinner. Is it anybody I know?"

Jessica felt the colour flood her cheeks. "Not exactly," she replied, feeling justified as the girl had never actually met her father. "It's somebody from work that's all."

"That's all!" Chellie gave her mother a hug of glee, almost lifting her off her feet. "You dark horse you. It's a man isn't it? Go on admit it? You've got a man coming to dinner."

Jessica opened the cupboard took out several potatoes and began to peel them furiously. "He happens to be my boss, Chellie." She glanced back over her shoulder, attempting to give the girl a warning glare, but Chellie was having none of it.

"Your boss? My, my, you are coming up in the world. After all this time you have finally found yourself a man."

Good grief, the girl made it sound positively sordid. She turned back from the sink and waved the potato knife at her. "It is not the way you think it is, Chellie. This dinner is purely business."

Chellie smiled at her and folded her arms. "A business lunch is it? On a Saturday afternoon? Come off it, Mum, I wasn't born yesterday. But there!" — she held up her hand as Jessica opened her mouth to protest once more — "I've been telling you for long enough that you should find someone to share your life with. Look at you, young, pretty, and fancy-free."

"Leave your mother alone, Chellie," Scott said quietly, speaking up at last. "You're embarrassing her in front of strangers."

Heavens, she had forgotten all about

Chellie's new friend. How could she, what must he think of them? "Forgive me, Scott, I didn't mean to neglect you. Would you like a drink? Tea? Coffee?"

"Tea would be very nice, thank you, Jessica."

"I'll do it, Mum," Chellie said cheerfully. "You carry on with your dinner."

"I am dear, I'm just peeling some more potatoes for you and Scott."

"No, don't do that, Mum. I wouldn't dream of interrupting your cosy little afternoon. Scott and I will have a cup of tea with you then we'll push on. Go to Macdonalds or somewhere, grab a hamburger then take in a film."

"No you won't," Jessica said firmly. "I can do better than that junk food. You stay and have a meal with us."

"I'd prefer not to, Mum." Chellie moved across and covered her mother's hand with her own. "We'll all feel uncomfortable thrown together like gooseberries; besides, neither of us has got a late pass so we couldn't have stayed that long." She smiled reassuringly. "We only ventured this far because Scott has got a car. You enjoy your afternoon, we will be perfectly all right."

"If you're sure." Jessica continued to look doubtful until the ringing of the front doorbell sent her in to a complete panic. A glance at the kitchen clock told her that he was over an hour early and she hadn't even had a chance to change into something more tidy.

"Go and let him in, Mum," said Chellie, taking her arm gently and leading her towards the stairs. "Then you can introduce us and we will keep him talking while you slip into something more sultry."

She ignored the sexual innuendoes and made her way downstairs instead; thinking how strange it was that father and daughter were about to meet for the first time and neither of them was aware of the fact. Maybe one day it would be different, they would both know, but not yet; she wasn't ready yet.

"I'm sorry I'm early," he began, as soon as she opened the door but she was hardly listening.

She was taken aback by how boyish he looked, dressed as he was in a pair of denim jeans and a pale-blue, short-sleeved shirt. She also noticed that the cold wind that had bothered her daughter so much, obviously didn't bother him, for his shirt was open at the neck revealing a sprinkling of dark hair. A shiver ran the length of her spine. She had forgotten how hairy he was. Yet how could she not have remembered how at sixteen she had loved to run her fingers through the tangle of dark hair on his chest.

"I'm sorry," he apologized, stepping in to the hall and closing the door behind him. "I've let the cold air in and made you shiver."

She turned away from him to hide her confusion. "It wasn't that at all.

I think someone just walked over my grave."

"That sounds ominous," he said, following her up the stairs with two strides to her one. "I didn't realize you were superstitious."

"I'm not." She stopped at the top of the stairs and turned to him puzzled. "I understood that was just an old saying."

"Maybe, but all old sayings have their roots firmly lodged in the past."

He broke off as Chellie chose that moment to emerge from the kitchen, and, if it hadn't been for the fact that Jessica was actually facing him at the time, she would have sworn that she had imagined the perplexed expression that shot across his face, for it was gone, as quickly as it had come, to be replaced by a warm smile.

"I'm sorry Jessica, I didn't realize you had other company. I would never have agreed to come if I had known I was intruding."

"Oh but you're not," Chellie chimed

in, before Jessica had a chance to answer. "We called in unexpectedly, but we're not stopping; you were the one with the invitation."

"We?" said Mitch, peering behind her with one brow raised. "There are more of you?"

"This is my daughter Chellie," interrupted Jessica quickly. "She called in with a friend." She turned back to her daughter. "This is Harry Mitchell, the man I told you about."

Mitch pulled a face, appearing not to notice the emphasis she had placed on his first name. "I hope she told you nice things about me!"

Chellie giggled. "She would hardly say a word at first; I had to drag the information out of her." Her eyes twinkled mischievously. "Still, I expect you have already found out how mysterious she can be."

When he turned back to face her, and said gravely, "I certainly have." Jessica felt her heartbeat increase to such a rate that she felt sure Mitch must be able to hear it from where he stood.

She quickly turned away and spoke to Chellie. "Take him in to the lounge, there's a dear, and give him a drink while I get changed."

"There's really no need to get all dressed up, Jessica," he protested. "You can see by my old jeans that I haven't bothered."

But she could see that those old jeans hadn't a mark on them and besides, she was a woman, she needed to look respectable. "I'd rather slip into something else, Mitch, if you don't mind, this dress is covered in flour."

"Mitch?" exclaimed Chellie. "I thought you said his name was Harry?"

He turned to smile at the girl. "It is, but I've been known as Mitch since my youth."

Was it her imagination or had he laid extra emphasis on the word youth?

"I won't be a minute," she said quickly. "You go with Chellie, she'll look after you." Then she hurried away, her mind in a turmoil. Why ever had she got herself involved in this charade in the first place? Why couldn't she have just greeted Mitch with, "How nice to see you again after all these years," and been done with it? It would have been over then, finished. Mitch could have acknowledged her or chose not to remember; either way she would at least have had a clearer understanding as to where she was going.

Deciding that casual dress on her part would make him feel more comfortable, she changed into a pair of black stretch jeans and a pink silk blouse. But, when she attempted to run a comb through her hair, she found to her dismay that the curls refused to be tamed, and sprang out from her head like coiled springs. "I'll have to do something about having my hair straightened," she muttered, peering with some dismay at her flushed cheeks and startled eyes.

Chellie was putting on her coat when she finally came back downstairs.

"You don't mind if we make a move now, do you?" she asked, dragging Scott to his feet. "We've decided on a film we want to see and it starts in half an hour."

Jessica frowned at her daughter. "You really don't have to go on our account you know. I'd love to have you stay."

Chellie walked across and gave her mother a hug. "Three's a crowd," she whispered in her mother's ear, "four is even worse." She turned back to Mitch and gave him a warm smile. "It was nice meeting you, I'm sure you'll enjoy the meal, Mum's a great cook."

"I'm sure she is. I just hope she hadn't gone to too much trouble. I could have easily taken her out to eat instead."

"There you are, Mum, a follow-up date to dinner. At this rate you'll be booked up for the next week."

Goodness, Chellie could be really embarrassing at times. She chose to ignore her remarks and hurried her down the stairs instead, before she made things even worse. "Now be sure to phone me next week," she instructed, ushering them both through the door. "Then I'll know when to expect you." They drove off and she closed the door behind them. It was then that it came to her that she and Mitch were alone.

Mitch was standing, staring thoughtfully out of the window when she got back to him; and she was able to admire the chiselled features silhouetted in the light from the window, before he turned suddenly and startled her with a question.

"Chellie doesn't look like you, Jessica. Does she take after her father?"

"Well no, not really," she was able to reply honestly, for the girl's eyes were much paler than Mitch's and her hair more mousy than black. Then with a hint of daring she added, "I believe she's inherited her father's sense of humour," for that was the thing that had struck her when she had seen them together for the first time.

"Oh, I see," Mitch said, and the blue eyes beneath the bushy brows appeared dark and haunted.

Jessica felt instantly contrite, for he didn't really see at all and yet she had obviously said something to hurt him. "Are you hungry?" she asked, deciding to get off the subject of Chellie for the time being. "I've made a steak and mushroom pie which should be about ready now."

He immediately looked apologetic. "I'm sorry, Jessica, I should have warned you I'm a vegetarian. I haven't eaten meat for years."

Again she felt the turmoil stir within her. Those darn years between them when they had lost each other completely. How could she have been expected to know such a thing about his lifestyle? And yet she still felt that she ought to have done, irrational as it might seem to an outsider. "I've cooked a good selection of vegetables. If you don't mind having those I could rustle you up an omelette, that is if you don't mind eating eggs?"

"That sounds delicious and yes I would like an omelette. I'm not a strict vegetarian, part of my diet is followed for health reasons. You know the sort of thing, low-fat, high-fibre foods."

A hand clutched at her heart. "You're not suffering from any health problems are you?" Surely fate wouldn't be so cruel.

He smiled and before she knew what he intended he was across the room and had grasped her small hands in his long, tanned fingers. "Dear, caring, Jessica. No, I am not suffering from a heart complaint, at least not the sort you have in mind. My trouble is purely vanity about my own well-being coupled with a distaste for eating anything that was once alive and kicking."

Jessica was having difficulty thinking straight with their fingers entwined together let alone take in everything he said. But she did wonder what he meant by the heartache he was hinting at. "I'm surprised you have a strong physique on the diet you follow," she exclaimed, without really thinking what she said, only knowing that she had somehow imagined vegetarians to be puny and thin, unlike Mitch whose broad shoulders and muscular chest were in perfect proportion to the rest of his body.

"Why thank you," he answered and followed this with a mock bow. "But meat isn't good for you, Jessica. We could all do with a lot less."

"But I like meat," she defended. "I couldn't stand to sit down to a plate of nuts and beans."

"That is where you need re-educating," he told her taking a step nearer so that she felt she couldn't breathe.

Just what sort of educating was it that he had in mind, she thought, letting her eyes follow the curve of his high cheekbones and follow through to the tip of his straight, chiselled nose. By the time her gaze had reached his full, generous mouth he had stopped talking and was poised within inches of her own parted lips and seemed about to kiss her.

It was at that precise moment that it came to her just what heartache he was suffering. It was over that woman Corinda had mentioned that he couldn't seem to shake off! It had nothing to do with her at all.

The instant it came to her she turned her head aside and the minute was lost. "I had better see to your omelette," she told him, pulling her fingers free and keeping her eyes averted. "Otherwise you will end up with nothing more than a plate of vegetables."

"That wouldn't bother me," he said quietly, but still she refused to meet his gaze.

"Maybe not but it would bother me," she said firmly. "However, since you don't seem unduly worried about tradition, I hope you won't mind eating in the kitchen. It's the only place where we have a table. I'm sorry."

"Why be sorry? I think it's a

cosy idea, I'm looking forward to it already."

And she could see by his expression that he was genuinely pleased. He obviously hadn't had much of a home life, she decided, if such minor domestication heartened him so much.

Jessica was glad that she had allowed adequately for the meal when she saw how heartily Mitch ate. She had suffered all her life with a gripping shyness about eating in company while Mitch had no such foibles. While she delicately picked at the food on her plate he made short work of the food on his.

Despite her protests Mitch helped her wash up the dishes after lunch and then she made coffee which he carried through on a tray to the lounge. He seemed in no hurry to get back to Franklins and seemed content to sit opposite her on the two-seater sofa and tell her of his plans for the company.

For her part she was happy to sit facing him on the smaller floral armchair and watch him as he talked, not really taking in everything he said but examining instead the strong, masculine features, sweep of dark hair and the set of his shoulders.

So intent was she in dreamily wondering what it would have been like had she let him take her in his arms, that she almost missed the question that he asked her about Chellie. It was only when she heard her daughter's name mentioned that she realized he had asked her something and she hadn't heard.

"I do believe you were almost asleep," he teased. "I hope I'm not boring you?"

She blinked rapidly to hide her confusion. "I'm sorry, Mitch, my mind was on something else. What was it you said?"

He leant forward on the sofa and smiled. "I asked you where Chellie was training?"

She was surprised at this sudden interest in Chellie, even more so when she saw how stiffly Mitch was sitting as he waited for her answer, despite seemingly trying to appear casual and nonchalant. "She's at Hendon," she admitted finally. "This is her fourth month, leaving her another eight to go before she passes through to the ranks of the big girls." She smiled at her own joke but it died on her face when she saw how seriously Mitch was treating the seemingly innocent enquiry.

"I would have thought Sunbury would have been nearer. I had a nephew who trained there; he said they had wonderful views of the river from the training grounds."

"Sunbury is no longer a training school," she told him, watching the expressions flitting across his face and wondering just what they meant. "They all have to pass through Hendon now, but she's happy there. Being a policewoman is what she has wanted to do since she was a little girl."

"She isn't much more than that now," he said softly.

Jessica was startled by the look of tenderness and regret that appeared in his normally hooded eyes. He seems to be battling with some inner conflict, she thought, feeling sorry for him as she remembered her own pain. Then it flashed back at her just how much of that pain had been caused by him, however indirectly or unintentionally. She sat up straight and, without meaning them to, the words came out coldly. "She may only look like a child, Mitch, but she's had a tough enough upbringing to be able adequately to take care of herself."

Mitch seemed startled by the force with which she spoke, and she was aware that it was due to her that he now got stiffly to his feet. "I'm sorry, Jessica, I appear to have outstayed my welcome."

She opened her mouth to protest then shut it again. What was the point? Mitch was a man who knew his own mind, despite the fact that she had virtually told him to go.

"Thank you for the meal and the company," he said gravely, looking down into her upturned face and ignoring the misery he saw written there.

His own expression remained closed and the dark eyes which a few moments ago had become animated and interested now remained dark, mysterious pools with hardly a ripple to tell her how he felt.

They walked down the stairs without a word passing between them, and long after she had closed the door behind him and heard him drive away she remained there; her back pressed up against the door and a weight in her heart that she knew only Mitch had the power to remove.

6

JESSICA had showered and was ready for work by 6.30 on Monday morning. She was eager to see Mitch again having spent a restless night on Saturday and a complete Sunday moping around wandering what he was doing.

When at last she walked through the imposing glass door of Franklins at 8.34 she had made up her mind that she would try and put both her own and Mitch's past behind her and concentrate on whether they had any sort of future together.

Of course, she reasoned, as she walked along the corridor with head bent in concentration, he may well have already decided that there was nothing between them at all; that the rebuffs he continued to receive every time he made any sort of move in her direction to be more than friends, had finally put him off.

She reached her new office without incident, opened the door and stepped inside. Then she stopped to stare in pleased surprise. Mitch had tidied and revamped the office so it looked pleasant and friendly. He had acquired an antique mahogany desk and an impressive metal-studded, brown leather executive chair for himself, and in the far corner by the window he had placed a smaller more modern version of the desk complete with luxurious, padded, swivel chair for her.

The processor had been moved from the reception area to her desk and standing alongside it was a small vase of primroses. A lump caught in her throat as she walked across to the desk and fingered the small velvet flowers. It was a coincidence of course; he had obviously put the flowers there to welcome her into his employ, yet he had chosen the very flowers that grew wild in that special place on the

Downs where they had escaped to be alone all those years before. How could he possibly remember — yet how could she possibly forget?

"I see you have found the flowers?" Mitch's cool voice cut through her reverie like a knife and sent her crashing in to a whirlpool of emotional turmoil.

"A simple flower, but I've always liked them," he continued pleasantly, seemingly unaware she was in any distress. "They seem to symbolize freedom growing wild the way they do."

Jessica took a shaky breath. "It was a nice gesture, Mitch, they are one of my favourites too." God, she sounded so formal. Why was it she had to behave like a child when it was important to her to appear sophisticated and cool.

"I'm glad you like them. Did you notice I put your desk by the window?"

"Yes I did." On impulse she turned to face him. "Mitch I'm grateful for the trouble you have gone to."

She saw a spark of interest kindle in his eyes and, greatly encouraged, she continued to attempt to put things right. "The flowers, the desk by the light so I can work better, may be small gestures on your part but they have made me feel welcome and encouraged. I want to thank you."

She was unprepared for his next move which was to take hold of her hand and cradle it between strong, brown fingers. Not knowing what else to do she let it stay there, and at the same time she tried to concentrate on what his moving lips were saying while her insides were being somersaulted by the sensation of his caressing thumb on the palm of her hand.

"There is really no need to thank me," he said softly, bending his head so that her lips were within inches of his own. "I am just hopeful that ours will be a long, happy, working relationship."

"So am I," she agreed dizzily, hoping that the partnership would not be all work and this time would last a great deal longer.

Her eyelids felt strangely heavy and, as his head moved just a fraction nearer, she closed her eyes, only to be rudely awakened when he let go of her hand and moved abruptly away.

Jessica stood staring at his hunched back in humiliated dismay. This time it had been he who had made the move away and now she knew how it felt. She had been prepared this time to let him kiss her, had been able to forget for a few minutes that he was in love with another woman, but it seemed he had not been so ready and it hurt.

"Right Jessica." He plunged his hands into the pockets of his pin-striped trousers and turned to face her, his bland expression denying any hint of their close encounter. "I think we had better start on this pile of letters. The sooner we can get them sent out, the quicker I will be able to follow them up."

Jessica kept her eyes on his face all

the time he was speaking but until he had finished he refused to meet them and when he did it was only to mockingly raise one eyebrow and tell her, "If anything isn't quite clear you have only to ask?"

Nothing is clear any more, she decided miserably as she pulled the chair sufficiently away from the desk so she could sit down. How could he be so moody? She didn't remember him that way at all. She thumbed through the pile of papers Mitch had placed on her desk, but she wasn't concentrating and could not make head or tail of what it was he wanted her to do.

"Do you understand the letters?" Mitch asked from the other side of the room. "You have to type the names and addresses on the printed letter, and an envelope of course."

The matter-of-fact way he said the words had the instant effect of clearing her fuddled brain. "I'm quite capable of working on my own," she told him, glaring across the processor, whilst at the same time wishing he hadn't moved away just when he had been about to kiss her.

"Good, because I have an appointment at eleven which means I have to leave now."

She watched him get to his feet with growing dismay. She had been looking forward to working alongside him, now it appeared that he would hardly be in the office if the pile of letters she was typing were anything to go by.

He picked up a large diary and walked across to her desk. "This is something else you can do, Jessica. I want you to book in my appointments, but be sure to arrange them so that I have time to get from one client to another."

She glanced down at the book but she didn't open it. She would look through that later when she was on her own. "When will you be back?" She glanced up at him as she spoke and found he was watching her, waiting, but for what?

Even before she realized what he intended he had cupped her chin in his hand and brushed his lips lightly across her own. "I'll be back about 2.30," he told her, then he was gone, the door shut quietly behind him and she was left alone to wonder what it was all about. Wonder just what game he was playing with her emotions?

She placed trembling fingers over her still tingling lips and felt as if she wanted to cry. It was all going so wrong. Her need for years had been to find the man who had fathered her child and whom she had never stopped loving. Now she had found him only to discover that he was not the same man but that she still loved him nevertheless. Now what did she do? Where now did her quest for happiness take her, when he was so obviously playing with her feelings?

Maybe he thinks I'm an easy catch, her ruthless mind persisted. Being divorced with a child might have given him the idea that I'd be content with an affair with no strings. The thought had her sitting bolt upright while a fury began to simmer in her breast. Well if that was his little game he could think again, because she was having no part of it.

You have hurt me enough, she told him silently, I refuse to let you hurt me again.

* * *

There was no opportunity for Jessica to test out her new resolution that day because Mitch didn't come back to the office. When 5.30 came and he still hadn't returned she decided she would no longer wait for him and packed up her things and went home.

Whilst standing at the bus stop she found her attention straying to every silver car that passed. Whatever is the point, she admonished, in making resolutions if you have every intention of breaking them at the first opportunity? But I wouldn't get in the car if he did turn up and offer me a lift, she defended. Liar, retaliated her conscience, you can't resist the man, go on, deny it?

She couldn't of course, and the realization of this fact made her even more miserable than she had felt earlier, when she thought she had made up her mind to ignore him and his advances — sparse and far between though they might have been. Now she knew that she was unlikely to be able to do it made her more depressed than ever.

Would she never have any control over her life, she demanded? Would he always be there in the background as he had been ever since she could remember? Probably, she decided, as her bus pulled in to the kerb and she got on. She might just as well resign herself to that fact once and for all then at least she might gain some sort of peace of mind.

She glanced casually out of the window then shot forward in her seat in astonishment. For, following the bus, was a familiar silver saloon driven by — she peered at the car, yes it was him — Mitch!

Whatever had possessed him to follow her home, she wondered, tentatively acknowledging his wave after giving a furtive look round the bus to make sure nobody else was watching. Surely she wasn't going to have to put up with him accompanying her every night?

The answering beat of her heart told her that that was exactly what she was hoping she would have to do. In fact, the voice in her head told her, if he hadn't appeared at some time tonight you would have been very disappointed indeed!

She alighted at her stop, looking around and felt her heart thud when neither Mitch or his car were anywhere to be seen. So it had been a coincidence, she sighed, shrugging her shoulders resignedly and turning the corner into her road. He had probably only realized she was on the bus after he had found himself behind it.

"Hello, Jessica."

Mitch's greeting startled Jessica out of her daydream. So lost had she been in her thoughts of him that she had failed to notice the car parked a few hundred yards into her road. Now she regarded him with tentative suspicion as her previous thoughts as to his intentions once more flooded her brain. "Hello Mitch. I didn't expect to see you again today. I waited until just after 5.30 before I left."

"The temp told me I'd only just missed you," he agreed, unwinding his long legs and climbing out of the car to stand beside her. "Apparently she saw you leave."

Just showed how you couldn't make a move in that place without somebody seeing you, she thought uncharitably. She hovered uncertainly, wondering just what it was Mitch expected of her or wanted her to say. "How did it go today?" she asked finally, when it became obvious to her that he was not about to make any earth-moving statements.

"Not too badly at all." He leant against the car and pulled his jacket closer to his chest. "It is rather cold to discuss things out here. How about coming for a drink with me so that I can tell you the details about the new client I have managed to sign up?"

She stared at him in dismay. How would he react when she told him she didn't drink or that she wasn't over fond of public houses. The youngsters these days seemed to spend most of their leisure time in them and would consider her anti-social for not being the same. "I don't think I feel up to it just at the moment, Mitch," she told him. Then, when she added, "Perhaps you would prefer to come in for a coffee," and saw the smug expression on his face, she realized she had played right into his hands.

He turned away walked round the car and held the door open. "Jump in, Jessica, I'll drive you down."

"It seems a bit silly," she argued, walking round and getting in. "Just for the sake of walking a few yards."

"Nonsense," he told her, getting back in beside her and turning on the engine. "Why walk when I've got to drive anyway? Seat belt?"

She shivered as their hands touched across the proffered belt, and wished for the umpteenth time that she could get out of reacting like a sixteen year old every time they came in to any sort of contact.

"There," he admonished, "now you have gone and got cold standing about."

And she acknowledged once again that he was still the same old Mitch who never missed a trick. Ah, but he did miss recognizing you, said the relentless voice in her head, and she ignored it and concentrated instead on keeping her body stiffly away from Mitch's as they drove the few yards before pulling up outside her maisonette.

She had unfastened her seat belt

and climbed out of the car before Mitch had a chance to walk round and open the door for her. "I'll open up while you secure the car," she told him, fumbling through her handbag for her keys before turning and hurrying up the narrow path.

However, by the time she had unlocked the door Mitch was behind her and standing so close she could feel his breath on the back of her neck. She nervously pushed the door wider, stepped aside, and ushered him in. "It might not be very tidy." She gave a shaky laugh. "I tend to leave things until I get home before I tackle them." Why had she said such a thing when she had purposely tidied the place this morning just in case such a thing should happen?

At the top of the stairs she tried to usher Mitch in to the lounge but he was having none of it and followed her in to the kitchen instead.

"We can talk while you make the coffee," he told her, flashing her one of his beguiling smiles so she wondered yet again just what he was up to.

She put on the kettle and got cups and plates out of the cupboard, all the time uncomfortably aware that Mitch's eyes were watching her every move. She almost turned round at one point and confronted him. Asked him just what he thought he was up to and didn't he realize that she had feelings too? But she managed to control the impulse and behave almost as if nothing had happened between them.

And won't happen again, she told him silently as she placed the tray of coffee carefully on the table, that is, not if I have any say in the matter. Then he looked up at her and unexpectedly smiled and she knew that had their friendship indeed been new, without any past between them to speak of, she would not have been able to deny him anything he asked of her. Was it any wonder then, she thought crossly, avoiding returning his smile as she pulled out the chair opposite, that she

130

had got herself into so much trouble the first time round?

"So tell me Jessica," — he pulled the coffee cup towards him cupped it in his strong, brown fingers and peered at her over the top of it — "how did your first day in your new job go? Did you manage to answer all the queries?"

She bit her lip and shifted uncomfortably. How could she tell him that in fact she had made several errors of judgement and that the company was likely to have to carry the cost of diestamping a whole batch of stationery orders that should have been printed by the cheaper letterpress method? She couldn't tell him. Let him find out for himself, she decided airily throwing caution to the wind. He should have stayed around on her first day instead of going off on some fictitious appointment that wasn't even in his diary.

"Well?"

His brows were now raised and he was watching her expression very closely; she would have to be careful. She suddenly stiffened. Perhaps his client was female! For all she knew he could have been off having fun while she was trying her damnedest to run the business. "I had an extremely busy day, Mitch, no thanks to you." That was it, go in on the attack. "If you had at least managed to stick around the office for a few days so that I got used to the change in routine things might have, well, run a bit smoother." She watched his brows shoot up and cursed her speed of tongue. Now she would have to admit to her mistakes when she wanted to appear so perfectly capable.

He leant across the table and grasped her hand strongly. "Just exactly what did happen while I was away?"

The touch of his fingers were preventing her answering, and she wished he wouldn't look at her in that way; sort of kindly and condescending. She almost wished he would revert to his blank impenetrable stare at least then she would know where she was.

"I-I." Stop mumbling, woman, and tell him straight. "It was that account for the T. W. Ruxley Financial Consultants." Her head went up defiantly and she refused to look at him. "I thought a diestamped letterheading would be much more appropriate for the prestige of their company, so I altered your instructions." She waited with bated breath; would he swallow her story?

When she finally shifted her gaze to look at him, the amused look on his face threw her completely off guard.

"You realized of course that I had quoted him for both types of printing so that he had already agreed our costs on the letterpress version?"

She could only nod miserably and hope the difference between the two operations would not amount to too great a deduction from her salary. Still unable to look at him she only heard him scrape back his chair then he was round to her side of the table and once more he was tilting her chin, forcing her to meet his gaze. "You little goose Jessica, admit that it was all a mistake. I won't mind; we all make them."

She trembled. Damn the man for having such an effect on her. Perhaps if she had taken notice of what Chellie had told her and mixed more she wouldn't suffer this dilemma every time somebody of the opposite sex touched her. Not anybody, Jessica, the voice told her, just Mitch.

"Why you're trembling," he exclaimed.

To her dismay he pulled her to her feet and gathered her protectively in his arms. Now she couldn't think straight cradled against his chest with her chin rubbing against his rough wool jacket.

He put her from him, held her at arm's length, and regarded her as if she were a child. "I will never be angry with you for using your initiative," he soothed. "We all make mistakes — I'm certainly no exception."

Her eyes narrowed slightly. Was she mistaken or had he laid a slight emphasis on the latter statement? Then before she had time to work out anything at all, he pulled her head back towards him and his mouth closed over hers.

7

JESSICA attempted to struggle at first, partly because she felt it was expected of her and partly because it felt strange being back in a man's arms. Then she relaxed and gave herself up to the heady feeling of being back where she belonged and everything being right with her world.

"Jessica," he whispered against her lips. "Dear, Jessica."

She wound her arms around his neck and pressed her body closer to his. He was warm, comfortable, and safe, like a lifelong friend. Her body was responding, tingling, coming alive beneath his touch. She felt dizzy, would have done almost anything he asked of her, then she was rudely awakened by Mitch pushing her roughly from him.

"I'm sorry, Jessica," he apologized. "I shouldn't have taken such a liberty.

It won't happen again I promise you, not until we've got to understand each other really well and know it's what we both want."

She could only stare at him in abject dismay. How could she tell him it was just what she did want when only a short time ago she had been telling herself he was up to no good? She couldn't tell him. She couldn't answer. She could only turn away pick up the cups and walk across to the sink.

"Are you angry with me, Jessica?"

She stiffened as the words brushed the back of her neck and made the hair there stand on end. He was standing too close. How did he expect her to answer or even think rationally with his body within inches of her own. "No, Mitch," she managed finally. "I'm not angry. At least not with you."

"Then don't be angry with yourself either," he ordered, taking hold of her shoulders and forcing her round to face him. "Circumstances have pushed us together, don't let's make the mistake others have made by rushing things between us."

It was us, Mitch, cried her silent voice. The two of us who rushed things before we were ready and then only I who suffered because of it. Yet how could he be expected to know that she was only angry with herself because she hadn't told him from the start who she was. Angry that she had ever started this charade that was now going so miserably wrong and effectively driving a wedge between then.

She turned away from him so that her expressive face wouldn't show him how mixed up she felt. But he still stood beside her, so near, yet so far apart.

"I'd like to take you out, Jessica," he said finally.

She picked up a teacloth and began to furiously rub the cups dry, yet all the time listening to what he had to say.

"I thought that perhaps if we got away from Franklins for a while we would both be far more relaxed.

Jessica?" His voice dropped in tone. "What do you think?"

What did she think? She turned back to face him, both the cup and towel still clutched in her hand. "You don't have to be nice to me, Mitch," she told him, ignoring the expression of surprise written across his face. "I've been looking after myself for a long time. I'm a big girl now I can manage." Then she walked across to the dresser and deposited the cups on their surface. Wallowing in her own misery she didn't hear Mitch silently cross the room and he again took her by surprise.

He grasped her shoulders and turned her firmly to face him. "Why are you persisting in this hostility, Jessica? I want us to be friends. Don't you like me? Is that it?" He let go of one shoulder to run an agitated hand through smooth, dark hair so that it became ruffled and made him appear somehow more vulnerable.

If only he knew how much she liked him, she thought wryly, then she would have no resistance whatsoever. She pulled herself up sharply, that was something she could not afford to let happen. Things were bad enough between them as it was. "How can I know if I like you," she said matter of factly. "I don't even know you." And she knew she spoke the truth, for after all these years how could he be anything more than a stranger?

"That's just what I want to put right." His hand returned to her shoulder, and he stared at her eagerly. "I'll take you out somewhere. How about Saturday? We could go for a nice drive and have a meal somewhere. Well, Jessica, what do you say?"

Her spirits rose then she remembered Chellie and they plunged once more. "I can't, Mitch, not this week." She watched his face darken and added hurriedly, "Chellie is coming home for the weekend. I can't let her down by not being here."

"Surely she can look after herself, Jessica?" He grinned. "In fact she might be grateful for the house to herself if she brings that fellow, Scott, home as well."

Jessica pulled her five-and-a-half-foot frame up to full height and glowered at him. "She is unlikely to bring a boy home to stay. Why, she had only just met him as far as I know." How dare he think such things of her daughter!

"Dear, Jessica, such a little innocent. The girls today are different from our time."

"Your time," she corrected, giving an exaggerated sniff, then wished she hadn't brought up their age differences.

Mitch appeared not to notice and carried on regardless. "I doubt if Chellie will thank you for your concern. After all she is about to become one of Her Majesty's law enforcers."

"You are probably right," she agreed, adding, "but I intend to be here for her anyway," and thereby put an end to the argument.

Mitch sighed. "Then it will have to be the week after. Will that suit you or have you got plans for that week too?"

"I'll let you know nearer the time." Why was he being so persistent about this date? "We will be working together so there will be plenty of opportunity of discussing it further. Now, would you like to stay and have something to eat?"

A look of disappointment swept over his face and he said abruptly, "No, Jessica, I'm sorry I can't. I've got to go out somewhere this evening."

And immediately she was on her guard, wondering where he was going and who with. I'm behaving like a jealous shrew, she thought with some amusement. Still she did have more claim to him than anybody else, even if he was unaware of the fact.

★ ★ ★

The week passed steadily for Jessica as she learnt in more detail the work involved in a small printers.

Most of her time was spent alone in the small office while Mitch visited clients in an attempt to build up the business. This meant that she was the one who answered the men's queries and telephoned the clients to confirm that the details which were not quite clear on their orders, were in fact correct. She found the learning process absorbing and by the time the week drew to an end was able to distinguish between the different types of paper as well as the type of printing method used.

"I'll take you round the factory next week," Mitch announced, startling her away from the steadily growing pile of introductory letters. "You will be able to understand things more if you actually see the workings of the place."

"I'd like that," she agreed, taking the opportunity of clearing her desk for the day now he'd broken her train of thought. "It might be easier to understand the men, when they talk to me of working the job one up or double sided, if I can see the machines and methods."

Mitch watched her from the opposite desk his brow creased into a thoughtful frown. "Do you like working here, Jessica?" he asked suddenly. "I mean, here in this office with me?"

"I'm hardly in this office with you," she retorted good naturedly. "You're off out most of the time and I'm left to cope alone."

She watched as he pushed back his chair got up and strolled across the room. She continued to follow his movements in some fascination as he hitched at the crease in his trousers, plunged his hands in to his trouser pockets then perched himself on the edge of her desk.

"Just this one week cold calling has made a substantial difference to the company's orders," he told her, his dark bushy brows arched over the quizzical blue eyes. "The old firm has been sorely slipping these past months, what with Tony's failing health and consequent inability to get out there and do some good."

Jessica couldn't take her eyes off his face; the animation written there when he spoke of the place fascinated her. He obviously thought a lot of his uncle she thought indulgently, then her presumptions were shattered when he leaned forward on to the top of the processor and rested his chin on his hands.

"I'm safeguarding my future, Jessica," he told her. "When I take over I want it to be a going concern, not a has been."

How callous could he be, she thought with a shiver, trying not to outwardly show her disdain. His uncle was lying at home ill and all he could think of was looking after himself.

"Don't look at me like that, Jessica." He eased himself off the table, walked round the desk and took her hand.

Now she wouldn't be able to think clearly, she thought wryly, as Mitch explained his motives.

"Tony, and his father before him, built up this business, made it what it is today." The pressure on her hand increased along with his excitement. "How can I let it fail now when there are so many men's jobs at stake?"

Put like that how could she deny he was right? Still? He did appear to be feathering his own nest, or perhaps it was a nest he was building to impress this girl he was carrying a torch for. The thought made her attempt to snatch her hand away but it was held fast. "You're hurting me," she told him, the indignation over the unknown girl reflecting in her voice.

"I'm sorry, Jessica." And he let her hand go instantly, much to her chagrin, adding, "But you do see what I mean don't you?"

She decided to try another tactic. To see just what exactly he was up to. "When is Tony coming back? Now Corinda is back she's been worrying me for work. There really isn't enough for her to do now that I'm helping you with your work. It may be that I'll have to move back to reception and let her take over." Almost as soon as she'd said the words Mitch reacted.

"You will do no such thing, Jessica," he told her, and his words had an edge to them that brooked no argument. "You are working for me now. I'll find something to keep Corinda occupied, don't you worry about her."

A frown settled between her drawn brows as she surveyed the man critically. "Is that fair, Mitch? Using her like this I mean? She has after all been with the company far longer than my few weeks." She watched the set of his shoulders tense and knew that her words had upset him.

He leant forward placed both hands on the desk and regarded her angrily. "Why must you always put me in the wrong? I'm doing what I think is best for everybody concerned, why won't you believe that?"

She returned his challenging stare warily. He could be a fighter when he chose to be, passionate when he believed in what he was doing. Of course, no doubt he always thought he was right. She decided to steer the subject away from Corinda and find out indirectly what Mitch had in mind for them both. She broke the eye contact between them and looked away as she spoke. "Just when is Tony likely to be back?" she asked, pretending to tidy the papers on her desk. "I'd like some idea of how long I'm to be working in here with you."

Mitch's reaction was immediate. He took the papers from her hand and forced her gaze back to his. "I thought you liked working with me, Jessica?" His tone demanded an answer, and she could tell that he expected it to be in the affirmative.

"I do, Mitch," she agreed, wishing the man wouldn't persistently hold on to her hand whilst expecting an honest answer. She didn't have a hope in hell of resisting him when they were constantly in physical contact like this.

"There you are then! What is it you are worrying about?"

"I just like to know where I stand," she insisted, wriggling her fingers in an effort to break free.

"You're not standing, you're sitting." A grin broke out on his face, but his attempts at humour fell flatly about her ears.

She was not amused when there were two jobs at stake, two people's lives — correction, three if you counted Tony's part in this charade. "Look, Mitch," she began, "You haven't told me when Tony is likely to be back. Will it be soon? A week, two weeks, a month?"

"Nearer six I should say."

His whole body came forward with his words, and she tried her best to ignore the close proximity of his lean, tanned face, knowing he was closely watching her reaction.

"Six weeks?" she managed, not knowing whether to feel pleased or apprehensive at the prospect of working so closely with him for so long.

"Six months," he corrected, smiling pleasantly. "Maybe not at all. He's got a heart wobble of some sort, been ordered to rest indefinitely."

Her eyes widened and two spots of colour appeared on each cheek. "The poor man," she said mechanically, while her mind whirled over this latest news that Mitch might be her new boss for good. She was rather sorry when she felt the pressure on her hand ease, although now Mitch had let it go she was able to think a little more clearly, unpleasant though these thoughts were turning out to be. For hadn't Corinda told her that Tony had wanted Mitch to settle down before he handed over the business to him? Had this latest ill health led to a change of plan or would Tony forego handing over completely until Mitch looked at least to be planning a more respectable lifestyle?

Her eyes went to Mitch, who had now moved away and was collecting his own things together leaving her to dissect this latest piece of news. "Of course, Jessica," he said suddenly, glancing over his shoulder to where she was sitting, "if you would rather work back in reception I can move Corinda in here and restore you to your old job, but I had rather hoped . . . "

He left the words unfinished but her heart still leapt in her throat at the thought of moving away from his side and back to her old job in reception. She couldn't do it, not now, and she had a suspicion that Mitch knew very well that she couldn't either if that cynical smile was anything to go by.

Damn the man for his self-assurance; he had upset her peace of mind years ago and he was doing the same to her all over again.

* * *

That evening, when she thought over Mitch's proposals for Franklin's future expansion, she was forced to consider whether he had any real feelings for her at all or whether she was just an instrument in his plans to gain control?

There seemed an endless stream of questions for which she had no answers, and yet it had seemed so simple through the long years, dreaming and wondering just how it would be if they ever met up again. Who would have dreamt that he wouldn't even remember her, that she would be unrecognizable from the mere schoolgirl she had been to the woman she had since become? Oh Mitch, her heart cried, I'm still the same girl inside, that much of me hasn't changed. Why, oh why, couldn't I have at least have made enough of an impression on you to carry my memory through the years. It would have been so simple if we could have started where we left off.

She sighed deeply. She was of course clutching at straws. Even if he had remembered there was no doubt they would have met again as strangers, have both changed through their own personal experiences of life as she was fast finding out Mitch had. Since he had not acknowledged her from his past, his insistence that she work by his side to the exclusion of anybody else must prove that he had an ulterior motive. He obviously wanted to impress Tony into thinking he was about to settle down, and was now responsible enough to take over the running of the company. Why else would he pay her any attention when she had no outstanding feature that would attract him?

She ran agitated fingers through the short, layered style that Chellie had insisted was modern. "You want to look with-it," her daughter had insisted. "Don't want them to think you aren't a girl of the world who doesn't know her way around." Now she wondered if the style really suited her small heart-shaped face and large, rather serious, grey eyes. Whenever she caught sight of herself in a mirror these days, she always appeared to look startled, like a young bird about to leave the nest and not sure how far it could fly or, in her case, jump.

But wasn't this much true, she asked herself? Wasn't she indeed still naive? Didn't the short, razored cut with the additional wispy fringe make her appear younger than her years? Wasn't it not a fact that if the picture she was painting of Mitch as the hard-bitten man of business was true then he might be just as likely to have decided to take advantage of these traits and use her as his new image of respectability?

The thought was not at all pleasant but it was one she had to face. Why else had he chosen her above Corinda who was also available and professed to like him? She, after all, would have been a more sensible choice since she was already well versed with the job?

Ah, she argued, but Corinda also knew what he was up to! Hadn't she already pointed out how many girlfriends he had got through? Not to mention that special one who was out there somewhere stopping the man really caring for anybody else. Corinda would therefore know that any pass on Mitch's part would not be a serious move. All these factors taken into account it looked as though she had been the obvious choice, had played right in to his hands by applying for the job at Franklins those few short weeks ago.

She would put all thought of him out of her mind this weekend, she decided determinedly. She would enjoy Chellie's visit tomorrow and when the girl had gone back to Hendon on Sunday she would start stripping the walls in the girl's bedroom. It would take her mind off the man by keeping her busy and it was a chore she had promised herself to get stuck into for a long time now.

8

CHELLIE arrived at 11.15 the following morning and whirled into the house like a breath of spring. She was bubbling over with energy and happiness and eager to tell Jessica all that had happened since they had last met.

Jessica was thankful to see her daughter was alone. Much as she had liked Scott, having somebody else present somehow inhibited their ability to talk naturally.

"It's nice to have you back darling," Jessica told her, giving her a hug before taking the lead up the stairs. She paused on the top tread and waited for Chellie to catch up. "It will have to be the kitchen, Chellie, I've started to prepare lunch." She continued into the kitchen, talking to Chellie over her shoulder as she walked. "I thought a tuna man and green salad would be nice. How does that sound to you?"

Chellie nodded approvingly. "Sounds like a nice change from all the stodge I've been having lately." She walked across to the table and pulled out a chair, noisily scraping the legs on the lino as she did so.

Jessica paused from layering onions and olives on to the tuna-filled man and turned to wave her knife at Chellie. "How many times have I got to tell you to lift the chair?" she admonished, then paused and sighed deeply. "But I mustn't nag at you, not after I've missed hearing your noisy clatter."

Chellie smiled fondly. "But I have kept in touch like I promised I would."

"Yes dear," Jessica agreed. "But the telephone isn't exactly the same as having you here with me."

Chellie pushed back the chair, crossed over to her mother and helped herself to an olive over Jessica's shoulder. "Still, Mum, I'm here now, so what's new?" She paused in her chewing to stare at her mother, her eyes flicking critically over the slight fame. "Have you lost weight, Mum?" Her small forehead creased anxiously. "Your cheekbones look far more pronounced than when I was last home."

Jessica laughed and said, "Of course not, though she had noticed herself how finely drawn she appeared lately. She knew this was due to the worries she had over Mitch but at the moment she felt powerless to help herself or do anything about it. She patted the young cheek affectionately. "I should be the one worrying about you, Chellie, not the other way around. Now tell me all that has been happening to you, how the tests have been going and if you have any indication of where you might be stationed?"

Chellie talked non-stop, whilst Jessica continued to prepare the salad as she listened; chopping lettuce and endives, shredding carrots, and dicing potatoes and cabbage hearts, before placing them all in a large glass bowl.

At least she could feel secure in the knowledge that her daughter was truly happy in her chosen career, she decided, noting her animated face as she placed the salad bowl on the table. There had been some doubt at the beginning when she had wondered if Chellie was cut out for the job, or more, whether she was cut out to watch her doing it. But it was something that the girl had always wanted, and although she had been starkly aware that she would miss her, since they had always been together and very close, she knew now that the decision on Chellie's part had been right.

"Shall I make the french dressing?" Chellie asked, rising from her chair expectantly.

"If you like dear, though it will have to be lemon juice I'm afraid, I'm right out of wine vinegar."

"That'll do," she said cheerfully, spooning salt, pepper and mustard in to a small glass container. She opened the cupboard and began rummaging through it. "Olive oil, Mum?"

"Second shelf at the back."

"Got it." She emerged from the cupboard and proceeded to carefully add the oil. Halfway through this operation she glanced across at Jessica. "Who do you think I saw last week?" she asked, so casually that Jessica was completely off guard.

"I don't know dear." She smiled indulgently at her daughter. "But I can see you're going to tell me anyway, so who was it?"

"Harry Mitchell," Chellie announced, without turning a hair. "He was right there on the camp talking to one of my senior officers." She stared at her mother waiting for her reaction, and mistook Jessica's chalk-white face and transfixed expression to be that of surprise rather than the acute shock that it was.

"Harry Mitchell?" Jessica repeated, although she barely felt her lips move. "Right there on the camp?"

"That's what I said, Mum," Chellie

agreed cheerfully. "We had tea together and a nice chat about you and the rest of the family."

Jessica felt behind her for a chair and sank wearily on to it. "You say he spoke to you?" Just what was the man up to? No way could he call the meeting simply a coincidence.

"Of course he spoke to me. He spotted me straight away as I crossed the quadrangle on my way to afternoon break."

"You say he spoke to you about me?"

She nodded. "Yes he did. About both of us actually. How old I was and where I was born. He seemed very interested." She leant towards her mother a twinkle of mischief in her eyes. "Are you holding out on me, Mum? I don't want to come home one weekend and find the pair of you have eloped and I'm left all alone!"

Jessica took a deep breath and said with some difficulty, "That's highly unlikely, Chellie and you know it."

161

Whilst all the time her head was reeling with the knowledge that for some reason Mitch had chosen to seek her daughter out and question her about her past. Just what did it all mean?

"Did he say why he was in the area, Chellie? Or didn't you think to ask?"

"I didn't have to, he volunteered the information. Said he had to see somebody who was living nearby. A relative of some sort though I can't remember exactly who he said it was."

A likely story, thought Jessica, and yet she still couldn't see what point there was in seeking Chellie out. Unless? She suddenly realized that her daughter's eyes were fixed on her face, and by the way her feelings always reflected themselves there, she was not surprised when Chellie's eyes grew wider and her expression took on the guise of a fully fledged detective.

"Do you think he was acting suspiciously, Mum? Tell me, do you think he's up to no good, maybe swindling the company funds?"

Jessica relaxed into laughter. "Of course not, silly. What's the point in stealing your own assets?"

"His assets? You mean he owns Franklins? I should hang on to him, Mum, he sounds as if he might be worth your while."

"Honestly Chellie, you make the whole thing sound so cold and calculated. Relationships aren't like that." At least not in her book they weren't but who was to know just how Mitch felt about things? Hadn't she already suspected he was using her as a means of obtaining respectability in his uncle's eyes?

Chellie curled her lip triumphantly. "So you have got a thing going with him? Good for you, I wholly approve."

Jessica stared at her daughter indulgently. At least she liked Mitch. Good grief what was she thinking. "There is nothing between us, Chellie. You have got hold of the wrong end of the stick completely. It's a business relationship that's all."

"As you've just pointed out, Mum, in my book they are one and the same thing. Just a modern variation on the boss and the secretary."

"Really Chellie, you've gone a bit too far."

Chellie walked across to where her mother was standing and put her arm round her shoulders. "I'm only teasing, but I think it is about time you found yourself, shall we say, a friend? After all you're not getting any younger."

The young could be very tactless at times she thought wryly. "Thank you Chellie, that makes me feel much better. Now, enough of this nonsense, let's change the subject. I was thinking of baking you a jam roll, or do you think it might be classed as unhealthily stodgy?"

"Mum, I haven't forgotten that the reason you are still alone is because you spent so much time raising me, ungrateful beast that I am. And yes, I would love your delicious jam bake and to hell with the stodge."

Jessica stared at her daughter fondly before getting back on her feet. How she loved this child of hers. How she loved the father too. Enough of that, she told herself sternly, this whole business is complicated enough as it is without you making things worse by giving in to your emotions. But still she was forced to turn away quickly before Chellie saw the threatened tears glistening on her lashes.

"I don't think for one minute that you are either a beast or ungrateful." Jessica opened the cupboard and made a great deal of trying to find the pudding ingredients while she gathered her composure. It took several attempts to swallow the lump in her throat before her feelings were back under control, only then did she emerge clutching the flour, packet of suet and jar of strawberry jam. "Besides which, raising you properly was all I ever wanted to do."

"Mum, you're too good to me

and everybody else," sighed Chellie, turning, walking back to the table and sinking down heavily on the chair. "I think it's a pity my real father never came back into our lives. It would have solved everything."

The innocent words sent Jessica's heart leaping in her chest so she felt she could hardly breathe. She gave a sidelong glance at her daughter, wondering if she realized just how near the truth her statement had been? But the girl suspected nothing and was staring dreamily into space, her chin resting on her hands.

I'll have it out with him on Monday, she decided; find out exactly what he means by walking in on Chellie's life and disturbing our equilibrium. Though she was forced to admit later when she was alone in her bedroom and had time to ponder on the incident again, that it was only her peace of mind that was upset. Chellie appeared completely unmoved by such an odd move on Mitch's part and failed to mention it again during the rest of her home visit.

★ ★ ★

By Monday morning Jessica was all ready to demand an explanation of Mitch as to why he had intruded on Chellie's life. She had gone over the matter time after time rehearsing exactly what she was going to say but when Mitch actually walked into the office she found her resolve had vanished and she was unable to demand anything of him.

"Morning, Jessica," he greeted, "how did your weekend go?"

This should have been the perfect opening, she knew, to ask him what he was playing at. Yet seeing him looking so poised and sure of himself somehow threw all her confidence to the wind.

"Fairly routine," she told him quickly, then when he gave her rather an odd look she felt she ought to enlarge further. "I've been doing some decorating," she explained. "Chellie's room was badly in need of brightening up."

As soon as she saw the dark brows meet over the bridge of the finely chiselled nose she remembered her refusal to go out with him the day before.

"I thought you said she was home this weekend?" His hands were thrust in to his trouser pockets as he towered over her accusingly. "You told me we couldn't go out because of it?"

"Oh she was," she said hastily, "but she didn't stay the whole weekend. She had some revising to do so she went back to Hendon on Sunday morning." He still looked faintly aggrieved and she felt her own indignation at his attitude begin to stir. Just who did he think he was that she had to give him excuses for her movements? She could do what she liked without asking him. "Besides," she told him coolly, turning her back and pretending to sort through the papers on her desk.

"I don't think all this extra activity after hours is a good thing." She waited with bated breath for his reaction and when it came she was surprised to see how calmly he took it.

"I see," was all he said, though she had a strange feeling that he had no intention of seeing at all. And when he strode across and planted his hands firmly on the desk so she was forced to look at him and see the expression in his eyes she knew that she had been right.

He lowered his head so they were both on the same level and she couldn't fail to notice how violently dark the blue eyes had become. "Stop playing games with me, Jessica," he ordered.

She watched with the same fascination as one would a snake, as the words were ground out through perfectly formed white teeth, and for the first time she felt actually afraid of him. She had never seen this side of Mitch before and she didn't understand it, but she knew now without a doubt that he would go all out to get exactly what he wanted.

A shiver ran up the length of her spine and it suddenly struck her that perhaps he was playing the game as she was and that he did know who she was after all. With this train of thought came the inevitable question. Why then was he playing games? Unless? She stared into the rugged face, the face that had come to mean so much to her and yet which she now knew so little about. No, she tried to shrug off the idea, she couldn't believe that he would do such a thing, or would he? Was it possible that he had worked out that Chellie belonged to him and that by acquiring her he acquired respectability? After all, surely an illegitimate daughter, even one claimed so late in her life, was preferable to no family at all? It would surely also save him having to go to the bother of getting involved with another woman?

She didn't want to think such things but the ideas tumbled over each other as they fought to be heard, sending her mind reeling with the knowledge that if this was so then once his game was finished he would no longer need her.

She took a deep breath. "I don't think it is me who is playing games, Mitch." She suddenly felt icy calm. If she was aware of what he was up to she would be better equipped to protect herself — and Chellie. "In fact, I think it might be better if I moved back to reception and let Corinda take my place here."

She watched his expression harden, saw his jaw clench and his eyes darken. "What exactly has brought all this on?" he asked, and she was surprised to find his voice had reverted to its former business-like tone. But she wasn't fooled for a minute. She was well aware of the steel behind the words.

"I'd rather not say," she said simply then turned away. She had a strong suspicion that if she kept her eyes on him she would be cajoled in to saying something she might regret.

She heard his sharp intake of breath. "So, I am to be blamed for something over which I have no defence. All right. Let it be. But let us get one thing straight, Jessica, you stay here with me, not Corinda."

A wave of relief shot through her giving her the courage to chance a glance at his face before nodding her agreement. This was one hand she had played and won, for she had no real desire to be banished back to reception. The work here and the people it gave her the opportunity to meet were far more interesting.

★ ★ ★

The rest of the week passed without incident. Mitch was away from the office for much of the time and when he was there he was painfully polite. Jessica wasn't sure whether to feel sorry or relieved since when he wasn't there he seemed to be the whole object of her thoughts to the exclusion of anything else and seriously impaired her ability to concentrate.

In fact it hardly seemed to matter whether he was there or not, because by the end of the week she was worn ragged; she had no rest from the chaotic turmoil of a mind that refused to give her any peace. The only bonus, as far as she could see, was that with Mitch away a lot she was left to make her own decisions on the various problems that cropped up. In the beginning when she had come up against something she wasn't quite sure of she had sought out Corinda's advice, only to discover the girl lacked even more confidence than she did. Consequently she had shrugged her shoulders and plunged in with both feet. Which meant that by Friday she had gained a great deal of knowledge of both the company and herself, simply by using her own initiative.

Mitch seemed positively pleased when he strode into the office on Friday morning and saw how much she had achieved.

"I knew you were capable of taking charge," he told her, and she couldn't help but feel pleasantly smug.

After all this was her first real job of work after a long time away and she felt justifiably satisfied that it was going so well. If only her private life were showing just as much improvement but by the way the week had passed without any sort of move on Mitch's part it looked likely that he had lost interest and was sticking to his side of the bargain not to bother her.

How she wished for the hundredth time that she had told him outright from the start who she was. At least it would have given him the chance to decide from the beginning whether he wanted to form any sort of attachment. The way things were now, she didn't know whether she was coming or going.

There was also the question of Chellie. Had he found out or maybe realized who she was and was somehow trying to gain Chellie's confidence behind her back, or was his visit to Hendon genuinely a chance meeting?

Now the friendliness had disappeared between them there looked even less opportunity of getting questions answered, putting things right.

"Did anything crop up that you felt unable to resolve?" he asked, unexpectedly perching himself on the corner of her desk and flashing her a smile that made her heart flip over.

"There was one complaint that I didn't quite understand," she admitted, trying hard to concentrate in the face of this sudden renewed interest on Mitch's part and the way he was continuing to observe her closely.

"Oh, and what exactly was that?" He folded his long arms and continued to keep his eyes trained on her face.

His eyes seemed to be raking her soul, she thought uncomfortably. Why now, after a week of near indifference, was he attempting to renew the little that had existed between them, shallow and unassuming though that friendship had been?

She swallowed hard, tried to push the emotional trauma from her mind and attempted to return to a business footing. "It was Singer & Godfrey, the merchant bankers," she explained. "They are complaining that the ink smudged on their diestamped letterheads, when they attempted to take copies."

Mitch gave a snort of impatient. "I suppose you didn't think to ask what sort of photocopier they were using?"

"Well, no," she replied, eyes wide.

To her disappointment he eased himself from her desk and paced the floor. "These big companies won't learn. I made the point of having questionnaires printed up to cover all these points, then they go and invest in new equipment and plunge us into the wrong."

Jessica stared at him baffled. "I don't understand, Mitch. If we have used the wrong ink in the printing then surely it is our fault?"

He turned back to her, and before she knew what he was about to do, her chin was cupped in his strong, brown fingers and his face was close to hers. "Dear Jessica, I keep forgetting how little time you have been here." Then his face softened and for a few seconds she was actually seeing through the blue windows to the man beyond as he told her, "Perhaps because it seems as though I have known you forever."

Then he let her go and abruptly turned away, leaving her to wonder if there was some sort of hidden message in the statement, or if she had imagined the longing she had seen written in his eyes.

"The trouble is, Jessica," he attempted to explain, "the water-based inks used for diestamping, tend to melt under the heat of these newfangled laser photocopies." He paused in his pacing to ponder. His finger thoughtfully tapping his chin. Then he turned to face her, his expression formal, slightly restrained. "I think a letter in that vein would be appropriate. Perhaps asking politely what sort of copiers they use rather than suggesting that this is indeed the cause." Then he smiled gently before adding, "But there, Jessica, I don't have to tell you how to word it, I'm sure you will be tact itself." And she knew somehow that things would be all right between them. That somehow they would work them out.

Consequently, when he turned to her ten minutes later and said to her casually, "That invitation from last week, Jessica, for a meal and drive on Saturday. It still stands. Do you want to go?"

She had no hesitation in replying, "Yes, Mitch. I'd love to," and letting her heart rule her head.

9

WHEN Saturday dawned it was bright and clear. The sort of day, thought Jessica, peering out through half-open curtains at the shared garden below, that really spelled out that spring was here at last.

The thought of spending the whole day in Mitch's company had got Jessica out of bed almost as soon as her eyes were open, and it brought home to her that this was the first weekend she had looked forward to since Chellie had gone away. To think that Mitch was responsible for her exhilaration was a little frightening.

She hummed happily to herself as she showered and pondered over what to wear, resolutely ignoring the recriminative warnings that were abounding in her head. She would enjoy today, she decided firmly, holding up a lemon striped shirt still on its hanger, against her chest and peering at her reflection. Perhaps they could forget their differences for a while and just take the day as it came, talk a while, laugh a little.

Her reflection frowned back at her, prompting her to discard the lemon cotton in favour of a pale, cornflower-sprigged silk. Yellow made her look too jaundiced, she decided, reaching in the wardrobe for her navy, knife-pleated skirt and white sandals to complete the outfit. At least this colour took attention away from the pale greyness of her eyes and injected a bit of colour into them.

With the latter in mind she chose a blue eyeshadow and added a hint of colour to her lips. In normal circumstances she didn't wear lipstick but her normally pale complexion appeared even more wan than usual, in her eyes, and called for a bit of drastic action. She even persuaded her hair to behave and managed to style the razor cut into layers which attractively framed her heart-shaped face, so that when Mitch rang the doorbell promptly at eleven, she was fairly satisfied with her appearance.

Mitch's eyes swept over her approvingly, lingering for a few seconds on her feet clad in the white sandals with their shapely two-inch heels before shrugging and looking back to her face with a pleased smile.

"You look wonderful, Jessica, as always," he told her, and she felt her spirits lift in response.

As he walked round the car and held open the door she noted his choice of dress was casual yet smart. Navy slacks neatly creased, topped by a crisp, pale-blue shirt and white cable cardigan ribbed in dark blue.

How strange that they should both choose the same colours, she thought, as she climbed into the seat and proceeded to fasten her seat belt. She turned to Mitch as he got in beside her. "Have you decided where we are going?" she asked him, and was slightly perturbed by the wry twist of his mouth and the strange answer he gave her.

"Oh yes, Jessica. I decided a long time ago where it would be."

She stared at the neatly groomed head for a few seconds longer before turning her eyes frontwards and puzzling over what his words meant. Then she gave up, shrugged her shoulders, and decided that he was probably referring to the fact that it had been a few weeks since she had taken up his offer and agreed to come out with him.

She settled back in her seat to enjoy the journey and realized they were heading out of town towards the countryside. Perhaps he knew of a country pub somewhere where they would eat, she decided, which would be rather a nice change from the restaurants she and Chellie sometimes ate in on birthdays and such.

She saw fields being ploughed, seeds sown and cattle grazing as they motored along, and from time to time she stole a glance at Mitch and was more than a little disconcerted to find that most of these glances revealed his mouth was set in a determined line. On one such occasion when he turned to her unexpectedly and caught her puzzled stare his expression relaxed slightly and for a few seconds the shadows were chased from his eyes.

"Would you like me to turn on the radio?" he asked, then, without waiting for her answer, he pressed the button, filling the car with soft music and dispelling any obligation on his part to talk to her.

She shivered, turned back to the window and concentrated on the passing scenery instead. What was the matter with him? Why was he acting in such a strange way? She didn't understand this at all. There was obviously something bothering him and no doubt before the day was out she would find out what it was. Would it however, be at the end of the day and spoil the hours between?

She shot up in her seat and stared at the rickety old sign ahead with its small wooden arm pointing at a tangent to the left. She knew what it said, even before they were close enough for her to read the worn, black lettering. Knew that it proclaimed Primrose Hill to be a quarter of a mile along the narrow country lane, beneath whose brow the Downs nestled before spreading out neatly like a patchwork quilt of greens and yellows.

She turned to Mitch and stared at him incredulously, but he was sitting straight backed, eyes front, concentrating on the road ahead. She clasped her hands together nervously, wondering what it all meant. Puzzled over why Mitch had brought her here when it held such painful memories for them both. Then she realized how foolish she was being, how unlikely he was to even remember a few stolen moments with an innocent young girl; one who was hardly aware of what she was doing or what the consequences would be.

But she had known, her heart cried out, she had known what she was doing but loving him had made everything seem right.

"I thought we would have a picnic," he said crisply, breaking the silence between them and giving her a cynical smile.

"A picnic?" she echoed, staring at him as if he was quite mad, as indeed she thought at this minute he was.

"That's right — a picnic." He again followed his words with a smile, that same little sardonic curl of his lips that made her stomach turn over and a nervous lump catch in her throat.

"Isn't it a little early in the season?" she attempted, glancing down at the cropped jacket, merely thrown over her scanty blouse and skirt as an afterthought.

But he dismissed her protests with an arrogant shrug of his broad shoulders. "Never too early," he told her. "But you'll have to walk from here. No cars allowed any closer to the Downs."

So her fears were justified, she thought with some dismay, as she obeyed his instructions took his offered hand and let him help her out of the car. He was taking her to the very spot, their very own place where, where . . . She couldn't bear to even think it, but she must. Her mind relentlessly reformed the memory of the place — to the time when Chellie was conceived!

"Is something the matter?" he asked, his tone pleasantly polite.

She stared up at him, the torture stark in her eyes but he appeared not to notice. "No," she denied, feeling a stab of misery pierce her soul. "Nothing that you would understand." She looked away from him, hating him for not remembering the moments that were locked for ever in her heart.

"Good, because I think you'll like this place. I often come here, it's a favourite of mine."

How could he? To think he often

came here, with — with, others. She couldn't bear it. The pain was so intense she felt her insides would split in two. Oh, Mitch, her heart cried out silently to him. I bore you a child and you let me carry the burden all these years and now you have taken away my dreams by not even remembering what I looked like.

"Are you feeling all right, Jessica?" he asked, showing no concern for her discomfort at all. "You look a little pale."

"I'm OK," she muttered miserably. Then added, "Just a little cold that's all," as a futile attempt at getting him to change his mind and take her somewhere else.

"I'll soon have you warmed up." His tone was still cheerfully determined and her heart sank even further when he added, "The place we are making for is still a brisk five-minute walk away." For she knew then that it was indeed the place she thought never to see again.

She watched in silent misery as he locked up the car, opened the boot and lifted out a square wicker basket.

"Right then, Jessica, off we go."

And he took hold of her arm and proceeded to lead her forward through the trees while she dragged her feet miserably beside him making no effort to keep up.

At first he seemed oblivious to her reluctance to make any headway, then he stopped suddenly and she cannoned into him, momentarily thrown off balance.

He stared down at her feet. "I knew those shoes were going to be unsuitable," he told her, dark brows arched over angry, glaring eyes which continued to glare accusingly at the offending sandals.

How dare he blame her, she thought, and for the first time since they had arrived on the Downs she felt her spirit rising above the inner turmoil. "If you had thought to tell me where we going I could have dressed accordingly." She ground the words at him, but he didn't appear to be the least put out.

"That much wasn't in my plans," he told her, and proceeded to walk on, once more dragging her along beside him, while she continued to wonder dismally, exactly what it was his words meant and what his motives were?

They approached the section of the Downs that held her memories, all too soon. Even from the distance they still had to go, she could see the abundance of yellow that heralded the primrose and which echoed her first thoughts of the day, that spring had really arrived.

"This is it," Mitch said softly, letting go of her arm and depositing the basket on the flower-strewn grass before plunging his hands deeply in to the pockets of his navy slacks.

Jessica could only continue to stare, through eyes misty with unshed tears; her heart and face miserable in the shadow of the cloudy midday sun. "Oh Mitch," she whispered, not meaning him to hear. "Why have you done this to me?"

But he heard the muttered words. Turned to her angrily and grasped her by the shoulders, his once expressionless features now alive with passion and feeling. "Why have I done what, Jess?" he demanded, tightening the pressure on her shoulders and making them ache. "I don't think you are being exactly fair do you? You have been the one holding out, not me. Perhaps now that I have brought you here you will admit that you know me? Acknowledge that we were lovers? Tell me that Chellie is indeed my child?"

She was startled into submission. Stampeded in to admitting with a mere nod of her head that everything Mitch said was indeed true. But even as she told him she could feel her spirit lift as her heart soared skywards like a freed bird. He had remembered her, their moments together; it was like a dream come true. Then she caught sight of his face and her heart plunged into a downward spiral, until it rested somewhere near the errant sandals.

"Why did you deny me knowledge of my child?" His voice matched the accusation in his dark brooding eyes, beneath which she trembled with fear and pain. "You could have told me, Jess. We could have worked something out together."

Even his reverting back to the use of her pet name struck her like a knife in the face of his anger. "But I was a child, Mitch. A young girl, reacting to the shock of becoming a mother in the only way I could think of. The solution was not to be found in you. You had already gone away. Even the enquiries were difficult. I didn't even know your full name despite us being acquainted through my uncle. How else was I supposed to react other than in panic?"

"Mickie would have found me, told me; he was your uncle you could have confided in him."

She stared at him as if he had

grown horns. "Don't be stupid, Mitch. I was barely sixteen. Mickie would have ridiculed a friendship with a man so much older. Would have been ready to have cried 'rape' if he had had an inkling of how we were." Her chin went up and she avoided his eyes. "I did what I thought necessary, exonerated you and married the boy up the street. He was young, like myself; only a few years older and not expected to have known any better."

"He was aware Chellie wasn't his?"

She laughed then. A noise that sounded bitter even to her own ears. "I wasn't in the habit of sleeping around, Mitch. Even if at the time you thought I was easy." She noted, but ignored his wince of pain, and continued to tell him word for painful word exactly how it had been. "The fearful truth that we were completely unsuited came later during the honeymoon and continued through ten long years." She raised her eyes to his then. Grey eyes full of painful memories of how it should have been and wasn't. And her next trembling words reflected the years of loneliness and longing. "Where were you, Mitch, when I needed you?" Then the tears came. Damping the fingers raised quickly to cover her anguish.

"My darling, Jess, I'm so very sorry," he told her, moving the hands from her eyes and gathering her up in his arms to cradle her against his chest. "I didn't know. Nobody told me. And when I came back from the assignment in America you were already married. Settled down and expecting a young baby, I was told. How was I to know that the facts were any different?"

"The facts, Mitch?" she exclaimed, resentfully, pulling away from his attempts at comfort and leaving wet marks in his stubbled chin. "Why did you always have to follow the facts? Perhaps if you had made a little more effort you would have found out where I was? Maybe been able to stop me making a mistake that was to last me a lifetime?"

"Not quite a lifetime, Jess. We've found each other now. We can start all over again."

His tone was eager, hopeful, the beloved face almost radiant. But? Could she start again now? Was it too late? Had she been too dogmatic in not acknowledging who he was at the start and now left it too late? "I don't know, Mitch." She turned away, a numbness now replacing the sorrow and stemming further tears. "Everything happened such a long time ago, it may be too late for us now."

"Look at me, Jess," he demanded, and she did. But when he pleaded, "Why are you torturing me like this?" she had no answers. For wasn't his pain also her own?

"I'm not the heartless person you think I am," he said brokenly, and she almost gave in. But she was a little too slow, and sensing her hesitance he gathered his pride, chased the old Mitch from his eyes, and reverted to the Mitch, whom even now she didn't know.

"Very well, Jess," he said coldly. "Have it your way. Believe that I never cared. But answer me one thing?"

"If I can."

"Does Chellie know your husband was not her real father?"

A hand clutched at her heart. "I had to tell her — there were reasons."

He continued to regard her coldly, while her heart cried out for his comforting arms. What are we doing to each other, she silently pleaded? Then Mitch's next words knocked any sympathy stone cold.

"That's all I need to know, Jess. This time you won't separate me from my daughter because I shall make it my duty to tell her who I am!"

She remembered the visit. "Is that why you embarrassed her by seeking her out at Hendon? Intending, originally, to tell her you were her father?"

"No, Jess, the answer is no on both counts. She wasn't put out, she was

195

pleased to see me. We had quite a long, enlightening talk."

She blinked rapidly, feeling confused. Why hadn't Chellie chosen to tell her the visit had been an extended one?

"Besides which," he continued, "my intention on that visit, was merely to find out if she could have belonged to me. If the date of her birth coincided with the date of a very special memory I had of nine months previously. Which, of course, it did."

A lump rose unexpectedly in her throat. It had meant enough to him to remember the exact dates they had made love. To her, a woman, and a virgin at that, it would have been hard for the experience not to have been indelibly engraved on her brain, whereas to him?

She immediately hardened her heart. She could have been another notch on his belt for all she knew — and she hadn't known, of course, because he hadn't sought her out to tell her. Hadn't bothered to try to find her.

196

Add all this to the knowledge that he had denied knowing her when she had finally turned up on his doorstep, even given that she had denied him also, and she could quite easily let him go without ever seeing him again.

"I want to go home," Jessica told him, turning abruptly away from him and walking back the way they had come.

"Supposing I don't choose to take you?"

Without slowing her step she gave him a derisory glance over her shoulder. "Then I shall thumb a lift," she answered, the firmness in her voice telling him she was as determined as her word.

He shrugged heavy shoulders, resignedly picked up the wicker basket and followed her up the path towards the sheltering copse and Primrose Lane.

10

JESSICA spent Sunday moping around the maisonette and generally feeling sorry for herself. Her mind kept going over the events of the day before, refusing to let her rest, filling her with regrets both about the way she had handled Mitch then and the situation all those years before.

The phone had rung several times and at first she had been going to ignore it; but the fear that it might have been Chellie prompted her to answer it, only to find that when she did there was no one there.

By the afternoon, when she had received three such phone calls, she had taken the phone off the hook, deciding that it was a fault at the exchange somewhere, positive in her own mind that Mitch would never have rung her and not spoken.

By the time it came to Monday she felt as if every nerve in her body was jangled and torn. She had gone over the situation with Mitch so many times that she no longer knew what they could possibly do to put things right between them. This thought filled her with more misery than she thought it possible for one person to feel. To have spent nearly nineteen years longing for the man of your dreams to return, and then to find you have both changed so much that you are now strangers was too distressing to dwell on.

Jessica blew her nose then once more got out her compact to powder over the tell-tale signs of her tears. She stared at herself in the mirror and her reflection stared back through large, tearful, grey eyes. How could she possibly go in to work, she thought with some dismay, as she examined the runs in her make-up and the alarming way she looked about to burst into tears? One sharp word and she would be off, and once she had started she would be unlikely to stop.

She turned away from the mirror to ponder on the situation. Perhaps she could call in sick? No, she dismissed that idea; Mitch wouldn't believe her and would be round here like a shot. The thought of being back on a one-to-one footing quite so quickly filled her with some alarm, she wasn't exactly ready for that yet. Much better to go to work and keep herself at a distance, treat the situation between them strictly as business as indeed it should be.

She arrived at the gate of Franklins with this resolve in her mind. By the time she reached her office the façade was already slipping and when Corinda walked into the room, stopped dead and announced in a genuinely concerned voice, "Good grief, Jessica, whatever have you been doing to yourself?" She wanted to turn straight round and go home.

But she stayed, and tried bluffing her way past Corinda, telling her, "It's nothing, honestly. Just a bit of a cold, that's all."

"It looks more than that to me," the girl retorted, refusing to be put off. "I've just recovered from a bout of flu and even I didn't look that bad."

"Thank you very much, Corinda. You've made me feel a whole lot better." Perhaps, she decided, with sudden insight, a few props might convince the girl otherwise, then she might just go away and leave her alone. She rummaged through her bag for her handkerchief, produced it and made a concerted effort at blowing her nose.

Corinda still continued to look unconvinced. She stared at Jessica for a few moments then her features softened and she perched herself on the desk, on almost the same spot Mitch himself always sat, which did nothing for Jessica's morale.

"You can tell me," she said sympathetically. "Although I think I can guess. It's Mitch isn't it?"

Taken completely by surprise Jessica moved the cotton handkerchief away from her face and stared at her wide eyed.

"You don't have to look like that. It wasn't hard to put two and two together."

"You might be making five of it," Jessica mumbled. Wondering just how much the girl had guessed.

"I doubt it." She continued to look smugly at her across the desk. "I've been here longer than you, don't forget. I've seen all the others."

"All the others?" she repeated weakly.

"Well . . . " She paused to ponder. "There was the one or two he took out to lunch. Purely business he said, but we knew differently."

"We?" This was getting worse by the minute.

"You know? The other girls. Those of us that were left that is. We didn't get the chance to even refuse. Mind you we weren't particularly sorry when we saw how quickly the girls left once Mitch had finished with them."

"So he actually had affairs with these

girls?" she persisted, wondering how much more she could take.

"We never had any proof, of course, and most of it was merely hearsay." Her face reflected a flicker of doubt at this point and Jessica quickly seized on it.

"I'm sorry, Corinda, but I can't believe Mitch would string anybody along, let alone a member of his own staff." She immediately began to feel better for having defended him, though why this should be so she had no idea. After all he had been ruthless enough with her feelings hadn't he?

Corinda got to her feet, looking suitably put out. "Of course you don't have to believe me if you don't want to."

"I don't want us to be bad friends, Corinda. It's just that I do know something of Mitch and he has never struck me as being dishonest about anything. Toying with people's feelings, is after all, a form of dishonesty."

"I saw him take the girls out," she

defended. "The meals were down on his expense sheet."

"Exactly. Business lunches as he said." She gave Corinda a coaxing smile. "He would hardly have drawn attention to the meals by claiming expenses and such if there was anything illicit about them, now would he?"

Corinda continued to look doubtful and Jessica had time to wonder why on earth it mattered so much to her that his staff showed him respect? The answer was, of course, that if he won credibility in their eyes it made his actions towards her look more likely to be sincere.

"I suppose you could be right," Corinda said finally, after much deliberation and with a faintly grudging air. "But that still doesn't explain why he never takes anybody home? Also, where the idea has come from that there is another woman somewhere, who had held him back from settling down all these years?"

Jessica dismissed the idea as nonsense

that the woman he couldn't forget could have been her. Much as it now seemed that Mitch had recognized her from the start, he had made no mention of even having given her a thought during the passing years, let alone pine over her. No, she thought with a sigh, that part of the girl's story could indeed be true, and who was she to blame him? He had believed himself to be free, after all. Still the inevitable pang of jealousy shot through her.

Corinda had now risen from the desk and was standing primly beside it with her arms folded. "I should warn you, Jessica, that the staff are already gossiping."

Her brows arched together. "Gossiping? About what?"

"You and Mitch! These things don't go unnoticed in a small firm like Franklins. You must have realized that much already?"

I'm beginning to learn pretty fast now, she thought, wondering if Corinda was the very one that was spreading all the rumours. "You can take it from me, Corinda, that Mitch has never taken me to lunch, business or otherwise."

"I'm not saying he has," she said hastily. "But it is becoming noticeable that he often gives you a lift home."

She gave Corinda what she hoped was a warning look. "A lift is not a crime. I'm sure had the other girls been the recipients they would not have been so quick to cry scandal."

"No, you are probably right," she muttered, looking a bit deflated. "I had better get along to my office now."

"Yes, Corinda, I think you had better," exclaimed a gruff voice from the doorway, which brought both heads round in startled unison.

Corinda scuttled past Mitch who promptly closed the door with a firm bang behind her, whilst Jessica did her best to hide her confusion.

Just how much had the man heard, she wondered? He could have been listening there for ages, heard her defending him like fury, and thought that everything was now all right. Well he would soon find out it was not, she thought with a certain degree of satisfaction. She had managed perfectly well all these years without him. If he thought he could come back in to her life and just take over, he had another think coming.

"I see Corinda is up to her usual fine form," he said smoothly, walking past her desk and across to his own. "Perhaps you now understand why I was not keen on having her working in here with me? She would no doubt have had us in the throes of a full-blown affair by the time the week was out."

So she was there merely to keep Corinda out? That was another blow to her self-esteem, especially since she had now to consider that he had known who she was all along. What was more to the point he had obviously been listening, had indeed heard what she'd had to say. The heat started to creep up her neck.

"So you usually listen at keyholes?" She gave him what she hoped was her most withering look.

"Sometimes," he said easily, continuing to watch her from across the room. "When there is anything worth hearing, that is."

"And you considered our conversation was?" She was conscious the heat had now reached her cheeks. If he stopped staring at her she was sure she would cool down.

Mitch leant back on the high-backed executive chair and put his hands behind his head. From this position he considered her question. "Let us get one thing straight, I don't consider anything Corinda says worth hearing, I never have. I would have probably warned you before that she was a gossip, but I'm in rather a dicey position being a director to suggest such a thing." He paused and appeared to be waiting for her reaction.

With a great deal of effort Jessica managed to keep her face deadpan and not give anything away.

He now moved forward on his chair, clasped his hands together and rested them on the desk in front of him. "What you have to say, however, Jess, is quite another matter altogether."

His use of her pet name made her flinch. So he was still intending to use it, she thought dolefully, despite the fact that there now seemed nothing left between them.

"In fact," Mitch continued, ignoring her lack of reply, "I did think that it might give me some clue to finding out just how your mind works with regard to relationships."

This statement did make her sit up in her seat indignantly. Just what relationships was he referring to? Certainly not theirs. As yet they didn't have one. "Now look here," she began.

"No, Jess, you listen to me." In one easy movement he was off his chair and two more strides brought him looming over her. As if still afraid she would escape he placed a determined hand on each arm of the chair, imprisoning her where she sat.

Her heart beat faster, but not because she was afraid of him only of what he had to say.

"I've spent a perplexing weekend trying to work out exactly what it is you want of me." He shrugged broad shoulders. "I've got to admit I'm baffled."

"What I want of you, Mitch?" her voice faltered, and she realized that he was right to be baffled because so was she. If he had asked her that same question any time up until a few weeks ago, she could have answered him truthfully. Now she no longer knew what that answer was.

"Yes, Jess," he repeated, "what do you want of me. I've gone to great lengths to play along with your little charade. Pretending, as you did, that we were strangers that had yet to strike up a friendship. When all the time we were old lovers with so much between us that the whole thing was ludicrous."

Her jaw dropped in amazement. Did he really see them as such? "Old lovers?" she grated through clenched teeth. "We were never, *old* lovers, Mitch, you know that very well."

"What were we then, Jess? Tell me? Because we were certainly more than just good friends!"

"Excuse me," she commanded, pushing unresisting hands from her chair, swinging the seat round and standing up so she could pace the floor in some agitation.

She stopped suddenly, turned and stared at him. "Lovers care what happens to each other, Mitch," she said with passion. "They don't disappear and expect the other one to face the consequences for their actions."

He reached out and caught hold of her wrist, pulling her towards him. "So that's what is troubling you, Jess? Yet I've already told you how it was."

"But you just don't realize how it

was for me." Grey eyes had come alive and now blazed in to his with unmasked fury. A fury she had not realized until now had been hidden inside of her. "I endured ten years of loneliness, yet not once did you try to find me." Her voice faltered as she bit back the tears and for a few moments she couldn't goon.

Mitch didn't interrupt the outburst but he had gradually pulled her closer, and without realizing how it had happened she was in his arms. She raised sweeping damp lashes and was within inches of watchful blue eyes. Watchful or wary? She wasn't certain, but she did know that for some reason she wanted to see pain there too. To make him feel a vestige of what she had felt while she waited for him to come.

"We weren't truly lovers, Mitch," she said finally, returning his gaze unflinchingly. "You were never really a father." This latter statement had the desired effect and the dark pupils narrowed in pain. Strangely she felt no satisfaction only a strong desire to comfort him, cradle him in her arms and kiss the hurt better. She didn't of course. She continued to keep her hands resting loosely on the bend of his elbow, while he did his damnedest to break down her resistance and pull her even closer.

Jessica watched in bizarre fascination as the dark brows jigged above ragged features and narrowed eyes as he fought to control his emotions. So intent was she at watching, that her stance slackened and before she knew what he was at she was completely enveloped in his arms.

"I could have been a good father, Jess, if you had only given me the chance." He mouthed the words against her cheeks, then his lips were on her eyes, her small nose.

She opened her mouth to protest, but before she could make any sound his mouth had closed over her parted lips.

Stunned, she didn't move but simply savoured the feel of his lips on hers, pressing, gently caressing. He pulled her closer and she could feel strong muscles, a firm chest, a sense of being protected.

The first euphoria was followed by a trickle of fear which ran from the top of her neck to the base of her spine, only to be greeted by a tingle of anticipation on its way up. She stirred in his arms, responded to his kiss, felt the years wash away and was once more youthful, carefree, a girl again.

She wound her arms round his neck, caught a tuft of wiry hair in her fingers, pulled his mouth down harder on her own and felt his probing tongue seeking between her teeth. She automatically pressed her body against him and was aware of the strangled groan brought forth by the gesture. She felt wonderful, alive again, and made no protest when his hands left the small of her back to seek lower, cup her bottom and press her firmly against the hardness of his arousal. She wanted him as much as he obviously wanted her, the taunts of *frigid* that she had endured had not been true.

They were so engrossed that neither of them heard the office door open or realized Corinda had entered until she gave a startled exclamation and muttered a hurried, 'Excuse me', causing them to jump apart guiltily.

Both of them, however, were well aware of her satisfied smirk as she hurriedly left the room, on course, they had no doubt, to relay what she had seen to the other members of staff.

11

"**I**T looks as though I'm going to end up as another statistic by the time Corinda has finished." Jessica grinned wryly, attempting to diffuse the situation. Why ever had she let things get so out of hand? She felt positively shaken, though not over the untimely entrance by Corinda more by the longing Mitch's touch had evoked.

"I don't see how," Mitch said easily, attempting to coax her back in to his arms. "After all you have no intention of leaving . . . or have you?"

She felt appalled by the idea. "Of course not," she said quickly, then on reflection added, "though I expect the other girls had no such intentions either."

Mitch's brows rose sardonically. "I thought you had defended my morals

216

where they were concerned."

She stared back at him accusingly. "You were listening at the door. How could you?"

"Quite easily," he told her, not even having the grace to look put out. "Besides, there was really no need. As you so rightly pointed out, I had nothing to do with them leaving. They had found better jobs to go to — that was all there was to it."

As they talked she had been backing away from his seeking arms. Now to her dismay she found she was up against the wall with nowhere else to go. "I don't think this is a very good idea," she told him, looking flustered and agitated. "Supposing Corinda comes back in?"

"Not a chance," he said softly. "She'll be far too busy relaying her tale to whoever will listen." He effectively pinned her against the wall by placing a hand either side of her head.

"Let me go, Mitch," she protested, but her voice wavered, sounding unconvincing even to her own ears.

217

And the steady beat of her heart had accelerated to such a degree that she felt dizzy and weak and unable to think further than the close proximity of his face to hers.

"I'm never letting you go again, Jess," he told her, staring into her eyes in a fashion as to brook no argument. "I made that mistake once, I don't intend to make it again. You're mine, you and Chellie, and from now on I intend to keep it that way."

How she had longed to hear those words. Now they had been spoken she was not at all sure that she was actually ready to share her life again. Then, of course, there was her daughter to consider. How ever would she take the news that Mitch was back, and here to stay? What had seemed a good idea when she had been a child might not seem such an attractive proposition now she had reached adulthood.

"You can't come back into my life after all these years and simply take it over," she finally told him, doing her best to avoid the dark probing eyes.

His lips cut short her protests and she was thankful, for she had no more valid arguments for keeping him away. He was right, they did belong together; the wild beating of her heart was proof enough of that.

With her back against the wall she could feel every ripple of Mitch's body as he pressed against her, was conscious of his strong masculine chest against the soft mould of her breasts, felt the pressure of muscular thighs against her sensuous hips. This was madness, utter madness, to behave in such a fashion in such a public place but she couldn't stop it, wanted the sensations his body was creating in hers, to go on for ever.

When reluctantly they finally pulled apart she could see that he was as shaken as she was.

"We'll have to continue this soul-searching another time," he told her.

And she could only agree, even if the agreement was a silent one. For she was an anxious as he was to resurrect and explore these newly discovered feelings of sexual arousal, which as far as she was concerned had lain dormant for too long.

* * *

Mitch dropped Jessica off after work with a promise to come back later that evening so they could discuss their future in more private surroundings. She watched his car until it vanished round the bend before unlocking the door and letting herself in to the maisonette.

She felt optimistic that they would be able to work things out between them now barriers had been pulled down and misunderstandings, to some extent, thrashed out. She was also looking forward to this evening, to having a cosy drink, listening to soft music and being held in Mitch's arms again, this time without being disturbed.

It was a heady feeling having

somebody who cared about you, she decided happily, as she discarded her suit for a wrap-around housecoat with short puffed sleeves. She had spent far too long in the shadows of her lonely marriage. Now that Laurie had managed to find happiness with somebody else, she was sure that the retribution was over, that she had paid for spoiling his life as well as her own and could now go forward.

Jessica didn't hear the ringing of the telephone at first. With the shower running at full blast every other sound was blocked out. She had also stayed under there longer than usual, going over the events of the day and trying to recapture the feel of Mitch's arms around her and the pressure of his lips on hers. The impatient shrilling only became obvious once she had turned off the pressure and stepped out of the cubicle dripping wet, to stand shivering on the plastic-backed mat. She hastily grabbed a towel, wrapped it sari-fashion around her wet body and hurried out to the hallway. The telephone rang off just as she reached out and touched the receiver.

Was it worth standing there shivering in the hallway, she pondered, hovering indecisively beside the green leather-inlaid table which housed the phone. No doubt as soon as she got back into the bathroom it would ring again; then she remembered the strange calls she had received on Sunday when nobody had been on the other end of the line. Perhaps they had started again? If they had, this time she would ring up the exchange and complain. For all she knew it could be somebody checking the maisonette to see if she was there with a view to breaking in.

The ripple of fear that greeted this thought was enough to send her straight back into the bathroom to towel herself dry. Still, she decided, at least Mitch would be round later to keep her company, which was some comfort at least.

She was almost dry when the phone

started again, setting the nerves jangling in her body and giving her imagination full rein. Without even bothering to cover her naked body she hurried to answer it and by the time she reached the telephone her trepidation had given way to anger. She picked up the receiver, dispensed with the formalities and shouted down the mouthpiece, "If you don't stop ringing this number — I'll call the police!"

"Mum, is that you?" Chellie's worried voice drifted back down the line. "What's all this about the police?"

"Chellie, darling." Relief washed over her; at least the phone now seemed to be working normally. "I'm sorry to greet you like that, it's just that I've had a few funny calls since yesterday."

"Well they had better luck than me." The worried tone held a hint of laughter. "I tried phoning you several times but I couldn't get through."

"Oh, it was you?"

"Probably. Was that what you were on about? The funny calls I mean?"

"Yes, dear, it was very worrying."

"I bet it was. I was worried too. You need somebody to look after you. I keep telling you to find yourself a man."

Chellie made it sound like looking for a lost dog. "There is a lot I have to tell you," she began, thinking of her and Mitch, and Chellie's need for a father. "When will you be coming home?"

"Not for a little while, Mum, though I might just be able to sneak a few hours off mid-week."

"If you could it would be lovely." as long as she didn't bring Scott, they wouldn't be able to talk then. "I could meet the train," she suggested quickly, just in case she had been thinking of using the boy's car.

"That would be a good idea. Now, I must tell you quickly why I rang. That boss of yours turned up again, completely out of the blue and making no excuses this time for being in the area."

An icy hand gripped Jessica's heart. What was he playing at going straight round to Chellie after she had told him to keep away until they had at least had the chance to talk. "Don't you like him, dear?" The words were out before she had even thought about what she was saying, and she could sense the puzzlement in her daughter's voice as it drifted thinly back down the line.

"I like him a lot, Mum, but I wondered if you thought it strange that he keeps seeking me out after just one meeting." There was a pause, then Chellie added, "I don't want to tread on your toes."

It took a few seconds for the implication of what the girl was saying to sink in. When it did Jessica was horrified. It appeared Chellie had already started to become attracted to the man, fondly imagined him to be a father figure, no doubt, and was unaware that this was where the attraction lay. "I'm seeing him tonight, Chellie," she said crisply. "I'll tell him to keep away; now you're not to worry."

"You're seeing him tonight? Oh, I see."

Was it her imagination or did Chellie sound disappointed?

There was a short silence before her next words startled Jessica into a stunned silence.

"I'd rather you didn't warn him off, Mum, though if you fancy him yourself I won't go with him to visit his friend."

Jessica swallowed but still her voice came out hoarsely. "What friend exactly has he offered to take you to see?"

"I don't know who she is."

So it was a she? A knife pierced Jessica's heart.

"All he said to me was that there was somebody whom he would greatly like me to meet and who would be delighted to see me . . . Mum? Are you still there?"

"I'm still here, Chellie," she confirmed, with some difficulty.

"And you don't mind if I go with him?"

What could she say? At least this way she would be able to find out who this woman was that he held a torch for. "I don't mind, Chellie." Then she added, "You are perfectly safe with him. He wouldn't hurt you."

The happy voice sang back down the line. "I know that much, Mum. I'm a policewoman, remember? I'm a good judge of character, besides, I think he is rather cute."

Why he had charmed her already, she thought startled; well, he wouldn't be so fond of himself once she had given him a piece of her mind!

"I've got to go now, my money has run out."

There was a series of pips followed by Chellie's hasty, "Goodbye." Then the line went dead in Jessica's ear.

Jessica stood thoughtfully for several minutes before replacing the receiver. Even after she had put it back on the hook and had walked through into the bathroom her mind was in a whirl. She mechanically slipped her housecoat over her now dry body, and walked out of the bathroom into the bedroom, while her mind refused to be stilled.

Mitch had certainly wasted no time in going straight along to the training school after he had dropped her off on Saturday. Or had it been Sunday? Chellie hadn't actually said when, and the telephone calls, which now appeared to have been Chellie trying to get through, had not started until Sunday evening.

She gave a little shrug of resignation as she sorted through her wardrobe for something casual to wear. What did it matter when Mitch had gone round there? The question still remained the same. Just why was he persisting in this obsession with Chellie before they had had a chance to get anywhere with their own relationship? There were many questions to be answered, points to mull over, feelings to consider, before she could even think about telling Chellie who Mitch was.

She selected a pale-grey dress with short sleeves, a button-through top and loose flowing skirt, deciding that the colour would reflect the battle in her eyes. Then she stopped, stepped back and gazed at the dress with some dismay. Did she really want to war with Mitch? Wouldn't it be much better if she forgave him and let them go forward from here on? For there was no doubt that this was what she was doing. Punishing him for not being with her all those years before.

Still, she decided, head thoughtfully on one side, the dress was sprigged with pink so it should brighten things up all round. Having justified her choice of clothes, she slipped the dress from its hanger, pulled out a pink angora cardigan from the chest of drawers, and proceeded to get dressed.

When Mitch arrived an hour later Jessica greeted him coolly. When he told her, "You're looking very nice,

Jess." She shrugged nonchalantly as if the careful dressing had taken her no time at all. And, when he took hold of her arm, pulled her gently towards him and added, "The colour matches the soft grey of your eyes," she stared at him in such an accusing manner, because he had failed to notice her agitation, that he would have had to be blind not to notice something was wrong.

Mitch held her arm firmly as she tried to turn away. "What is it, Jess? What have I done now?"

"You know very well." Her tone was cold and she was aware she was being unreasonable. For how could he possibly know what was in her mind when she didn't understand any of it herself.

He gave a drawn-out sigh. "I don't know, Jess. In fact I am beginning to think I know much less about women than I thought I did since you've come back in to my life."

"I have not come back in to your

life," she said indignantly. "Just because you happen to be a partner in the firm where I work, doesn't mean you have to give me lifts home or entertain me."

Mitch pulled her closer, held her firmly so no amount of wriggling would allow her to break free.

"It's no use struggling, Jess. Now I have found you again I have no intention of letting you go."

She stared up at him dubiously. "You found me again? Why, I bet you never even gave me another thought all these years? Certainly had no idea that you had a daughter or how I was suffering in the prison you had forced me into . . . " The latter words caught in her throat. Would she never be free of the memories?

"I wasn't your jailer, Jess." Mitch spoke the words carefully, whilst keeping his firm blue gaze on her face. "You chose to marry somebody other than me. You can't blame me for that part of it."

"But you weren't around, Mitch."

The words were driven out on a sob. "What else was I supposed to do?"

Mitch waited while she composed herself, allowing her to swallow back the tears, making no attempt to comfort her other than to hold her gently at arm's length. The only hint he gave of his concern was the crease of worry on his forehead.

And that was probably in case he was being misjudged, Jessica thought, feeling suddenly sorry for herself in the face of Mitch's apparent lack of concern. No doubt his sense of fair play was typically male, and mattered as long as it did not harm his male ego.

When Mitch was sure she was recovered he continued, "Nobody is forced to marry in this day and age, Jess. Although you obviously had your reasons. Perhaps it was because you needed the security of a husband or maybe it was because at the time you didn't care enough for me?"

She opened her mouth to protest but he wouldn't let her speak.

"No, Jess, let me finish, you've had your say." He paused, took a shaky breath, but his eyes continued to blaze into hers, affording her no escape. "Which ever way you look at it you denied me a daughter. I had no contact in her growing years; I now aim to put things right and see as much of her as possible."

A resigned shrug followed his passionate outburst, and for the first time his hold on her was slackened. She could move now, away if need be, but she didn't want to. Oh Mitch, her heart cried, I never want to move away from you again. "What about me in all this?" she cried out. "Why are you showing such concern for Chellie and not for me? Don't I matter too? Or is it just the child who was denied you, who is at the root of all this?"

She was instantly dragged back into his enveloping arms, held against his cheek and rocked gently. "Oh, Jess," he murmured. "Of course you matter. You matter a great deal. In fact, the truth of it is, you matter so greatly that I can't live without you. Can't bear to have you out of my sight for more than a short span of time, in case you take it into your head to vanish all over again, and this time I am unable to find you . . ."

He broke off from speaking as his mouth sought her waiting lips. But although she longed for the comfort of his mouth on hers the contact was brief, a mere touch of gossamer which left no lingering feel in its feather-like touch. His lips moved then to her eyes, and almost as soon as her lashes had shuttered to his touch the butterfly touch had shifted to the sensitive skin behind her ears then to her ears themselves to nibble and caress. Whilst all the time the words that he couldn't live without her, pounded in her brain.

Mitch continued to follow the line of Jessica's curved neck, reached the division of neck and shoulder and lingered there for a few minutes before following on with his fingers.

With a delicious fizzy feeling in her stomach, Jessica felt Mitch's fingers delicately fumble with the top button of her dress, then the second and, just as he hesitated on the third, a voice started in her head.

What about the other woman, it ruthlessly questioned? He is taking Chellie to see her, remember? She froze instantly, pushed Mitch's seeking hand from her body and dragged the front of her dress back to a level of decency.

"I believe there is something you have forgotten to tell me?" she blazed, glaring resentfully into Mitch's dazed eyes.

12

MITCH'S attempts to take Jessica back into his arms were thwarted when she turned away from him, walked over to the sofa and sat down heavily on the pink floral cushions.

He remained where he was eyeing her warily.

Jessica's eyes flickered across to where he stood awkwardly and steeled herself not to feel sorry for him. "Well Mitch? What have you got to say for yourself?"

Mitch appearing to regain his composure, thrust his hands into the pockets of his black, calico slacks, walked casually across to the sofa and sat down beside her.

Jessica offered no resistance when he untangled one set of fingers from the folds of her unbuttoned dress. Not even when he placed it on his thinly clad knee and imprisoned it beneath his own. It did mean however, that she was unable to think clearly since she could now feel every ripple of leg muscle beneath her fingers. The sensations were running riot with her imagination and she found herself wondering if the movements she could feel on the palm of her hand were vibrating right up his legs to his thighs and affecting the strong muscles there? The implications of where these thoughts were leading sent the blood rushing to her cheeks and she dropped her lashes in some confusion.

"Look at me, Jess," he commanded. "Or have I done something so wrong that you cannot bear to meet my eyes?"

She lifted the long, curled lashes with some difficulty. "Only you are able to answer me that question," she managed, trying desperately to steer her erotic thoughts away from Mitch's body. The suggestively caressing fingers on her hand weren't helping matters either. She made a futile attempt to free it, but to no avail. Goodness, she thought dismally, this was proving a difficult task, but then, after all, it had been a long time.

"Why must you talk in riddles, Jess? What is it exactly you are worried about?"

"You went back to see Chellie," she accused. "Told her you would take her to see somebody, another woman. That's what I am on about."

Mitch stared at her in stunned silence. Then to her amazement he let go of her hand, threw back his head and let out a roar of laughter.

"I don't happen to think it is funny," she said indignantly, hiding her confusion by attempting to re-button the dress.

He put a restraining hand on her fumbling fingers. "Don't do them up," he said gently. "I'll only have to undo them again."

She shook his hand off. "It is all

very well for you to harbour a liking for someone for years, Harry Mitchell, but to openly attempt to take my daughter to meet them is quite another matter."

"Who told you that?" he asked urgently, placing hands on her shoulders.

"Chellie told me," she said indignantly. "She telephoned and told me all about you visiting her. What hurt most, was her obvious growing fondness for *you* in the face of this other woman."

"I'm not talking about Chellie," he exclaimed impatiently. "Who told you I was harbouring some secret desire?"

Jessica looked up at him in surprise. "It was Corinda. I had hardly been with the company any time at all when she warned me about your flighty ways. When you appeared not to have any recollection of my previous existence, but went out of your way to make an impression, it all seemed to fit." She shrugged resigned shoulders. "When she added later that you had a secret love and that was why your interest never went more than skin deep, it made sense. You had not, after all, made any clear intention of anything being between us."

"Dear, sweet, Jess."

She could only sit woodenly while he clasped her in his arms, rained kisses on her cheeks.

Then he put her once more from him and continued to explain. "The only reason I didn't go too fast was because I wasn't sure what game you were playing. How could I not know who you were when I had held you in my heart for so long? Whilst you? You stunned me when you showed no indication of having known me, let Corinda introduce us, and merely acknowledge the greeting with a nod of your head and no kind words for my years of torment — "

She broke in then, she couldn't let him get away with that. "*Your* years of torment?" she repeated, eyes wide and incredulous.

"Yes, Jess, my years. Or do you

think you have the monopoly on strong feelings?" He grasped her hands tightly. "I longed for you, cherished the memories of our love, tried to find out where you had gone." The dark, craggy features shuddered with pain. "Once I found out that you had married and were having a child, I decided it wasn't fair to disturb your life, that you had obviously not felt about me as I had felt about you."

"How could you believe that?" she asked brokenly.

"It was easy, Jess." The blue-eyed gaze stared deep into her soul. "I was only a young man myself, still impressionable, very vulnerable in the face of my love. I made up my mind I was not going to get hurt again, and that promise followed me through the years, until you stepped back in to my life once more and I realized that Chellie belonged to me."

"What first made you suspect that she could have been, Mitch? It was obviously something you felt strongly or you would never have questioned her about her birth?"

His gaze softened. "You never met my family, did you, Jess?"

She shook her head. "That was the trouble with our relationship from the start. You were just Mickie's friend and consequently mine too — at least in everybody else's eyes. Anything more would have just raised people's suspicions."

He nodded. "Exactly. You therefore never even saw a photograph of my sister, Jodie. If you had, you would have seen that Chellie was the image of her when she was her age."

"Really?" She felt a warm glow begin to creep through her body.

"Really," he affirmed. "Jodie had the same small features and almost the same shade of hair colouring. Except for her grey eyes, which she gets from you, Chellie could be an exact miniature of Jodie." His eyes took on a far-away look. "Even down to the way her eyes sparkle and her nose twitches when she gets excited or is pleased about something. It gave me quite a turn when I saw her that first time."

Jessica felt a lump lodge in her throat. "You said *had*, Mitch? Has something happened to Jodie?"

Shadows scurried across Mitch's face and clouded his eyes. "She was killed by a hit-and-run driver a week before her twenty-first birthday." The painful memory was dragged from his lips in a ragged burst. "I was devoted to her, devastated when it happened. The driver was never found so he got off scot free."

"How awful," she muttered, realizing for the first time how he must have felt when Chellie walked into his life.

He gave a long, ragged sigh. "It was an awful time, Jess, not only for me but also for my mother, who had only recently been widowed."

"Your mother is still alive?"

His features relaxed into a warm smile which chased the shadows from his eyes. "Yes, Jess, she is. I think you will like her and I am sure she will be enamoured with Chellie, when she meets her, which is where I had intended taking her, to meet the *other* woman in my life."

"Your mother?" she repeated, as enlightenment dawned. "It was your mother you wanted Chellie to meet? How foolish I've been, how heartless."

Then she was in his arms, and this time there was a sense of belonging when on previous occasions the feeling had somehow managed to elude her.

"Not heartless, Jess," he whispered against her hair. "I wouldn't use the word heartless when you have brought up my child virtually single-handed."

"And named the child after you," she exclaimed suddenly, pulling back from his arms so she could see his face. "That is I gave her a similar name to what I believed was yours."

Mitch continued to look puzzled. "But how does Chellie compare to either Harry or Mitch?"

"Her real name is Michelle," she said gently, and was gratified to see the understanding dawn in Mitch's eyes. "I have always called her Chellie for short."

"And to think I thought the Chellie was spelt with an 'S'."

"That still doesn't excuse the way I treated you," she said passionately.

"I was just as much to blame." He pulled her back into his arms, attempting to comfort her. "I shouldn't have gone along with your little charade."

Jessica was still not convinced. "To think I acted like that after carrying my love through nineteen lonely years."

"You were just misguided in your judgement of me, that was all," he said easily, adding, "Besides at least it proves you have a heart." His fingers left her shoulders and before she realized what he intended he had slipped his hand inside the parted bodice of her dress.

A ripple of excitement stirred gently

in the pit of her stomach and started to move downwards, as his fingers sought beneath the soft grey cloth before closing possessively over her left breast.

"In fact, Jess," he whispered softly, his mouth against her ear, "I can feel it beating quite distinctly beneath my fingers."

Jessica didn't answer. She couldn't find the words to protest, besides which she didn't want him to stop. The sensations his touch were evoking were an exquisite stirring of delight which had long been forgotten.

Mitch lowered his head and stared into the half-shuttered grey eyes which were already cloudy with emotion. How he loved that small face, how this moment had haunted his dreams and how he now longed to take her as he had taken her on that day all those years ago.

Jessica stared up at him, increasingly aware of his hand still fastened around her aching breast with its nipple now hardened in response. He looks strange, she thought, and opened her mouth to speak. But immediately Mitch's mouth closed over her parted lips.

Jessica savoured the feel of his mouth on hers without moving, then, as she instinctively wriggled her body closer in response, she felt his tongue probing between her teeth, felt his body harden against hers and a shudder of delight surged through her.

"Oh, Jess," he groaned, "can you feel what you've done to me?"

He took her hand and placed it between them, and she could feel the intensity of his arousal beneath her fingers.

"You had no need to show me," she murmured against his lips. "I could already feel your body through the thinness of my dress."

"That's as maybe, Jess, but I like to feel your caresses; they excite me."

"You already feel excited enough, to me," she told him, and gave a nervous giggle, which failed to get past Mitch.

"Are you afraid of me, Jess?" he asked gently, head slightly to one side, expression thoughtful. "We can stop now if you want more time? Although it might take a little while to convince the rest of my body my intentions aren't serious!"

He followed his words with a concerned smile and immediately her trepidation vanished. Of course she wasn't afraid of him, she knew he would never hurt her. "It's just that it has been a long time, Mitch," she told him, staring up into his face and marking out with her eyes every beloved feature, from the finely chiselled nose, dark-fringed, blue-black eyes, through to the mop of unruly black hair; she loved every bit of him.

"It has?"

To her amazement he looked ridiculously pleased with the idea, although she noticed he didn't say he had also abstained. Still, she thought, sighing inwardly, he was a man after all and would no doubt tell her their needs were completely different to a woman's.

Mitch mistook her intake of breath for a further show of anxiety. "Don't worry Jess. I won't do anything you don't want me to."

But she did want him to, she realized, with sudden passionate longing. She wanted him to make love to her now she was a woman, the way he had made love to her as a girl. Of course, lying down amongst the primroses was out of the question but there was always the bedroom? Would it seem too presumptuous if she were to take him there?

As if sensing her dilemma, Mitch took a step back and looked at her expressive face. "What is it, Jess? Tell me? What is worrying you?"

She hesitated, then asked quickly, "Do you think somewhere other than here would be more suitable?" She followed her words with a sweeping gesture of the room, adding, "After all we have both waited a long time for this moment."

Mitch regarded her thoughtfully for a few seconds, then his features relaxed into a gentle smile. "Do you want us to make love in the bedroom?"

Jessica's gentle heart contracted at such a graphic presumption and she was only able to manage a quick nod.

Mitch, however, was not a bit bothered. "Then lead me to it," he told her, but when he added, "You shameless hussy." She was more than a little put out.

"I'm only teasing," he told her, when he caught sight of her face. "I know you have always belonged to me alone, and so in my heart have I to you. But a man's needs are on a different level, so I can't promise you that I have been quite as chaste."

A predictable observation on my part, she thought, as with Mitch's arm around her they proceeded along the passage to the bedroom; only pausing long enough to close the door softly behind them.

* * *

Much later, when Mitch lay sleeping beside Jessica and she lay elated and wide awake, she reflected on the summer of innocence which had moulded her future and given her somebody to love. For, if she had not had Chellie, she and Mitch might not have been together now.

Yes, she decided, reaching out to her man with a loving finger to trace the shuttered eyes, strong nose and firm chin . . . everything had happened for the best, after all.

THE END

WITH SOMEBODY ELSE
Theresa Charles

Rosamond sets off for Cornwall with Hugo to meet his family, blissfully unaware of the shocks in store for her.

A SUMMER FOR STRANGERS
Claire Hamilton

Because she had lost her job, her flat and she had no money, Tabitha agreed to pose as Adam's future wife although she believed the scheme to be deceitful and cruel.

VILLA OF SINGING WATER
Angela Petron

The disquieting incidents that occurred at the Vatican and the Colosseum did not trouble Jan at first, but then they became increasingly unpleasant and alarming.

DOCTOR NAPIER'S NURSE
Pauline Ash

When cousins Midge and Derry are entered as probationer nurses on the same day but at different hospitals they agree to exchange identities.

A GIRL LIKE JULIE
Louise Ellis

Caroline absolutely adored Hugh Barrington, but then Julie Crane came into their lives. Julie was the kind of girl who attracts men without even trying.

COUNTRY DOCTOR
Paula Lindsay

When Evan Richmond bought a practice in a remote country village he did not realise that a casual encounter would lead to the loss of his heart.

ENCORE
Helga Moray

Craig and Janet realise that their true happiness lies with each other, but it is only under traumatic circumstances that they can be reunited.

NICOLETTE
Ivy Preston

When Grant Alston came back into her life, Nicolette was faced with a dilemma. Should she follow the path of duty or the path of love?

THE GOLDEN PUMA
Margaret Way

Catherine's time was spent looking after her father's Queensland farm. But what life was there without David, who wasn't interested in her?

HOSPITAL BY THE LAKE
Anne Durham

Nurse Marguerite Ingleby was always ready to become personally involved with her patients, to the despair of Brian Field, the Senior Surgical Registrar, who loved her.

VALLEY OF CONFLICT
David Farrell

Isolated in a hostel in the French Alps, Ann Russell sees her fiancé being seduced by a young girl. Then comes the avalanche that imperils their lives.

NURSE'S CHOICE
Peggy Gaddis

A proposal of marriage from the incredibly handsome and wealthy Reagan was enough to upset any girl — and Brooke Martin was no exception.

A DANGEROUS MAN
Anne Goring

Photographer Polly Burton was on safari in Mombasa when she met enigmatic Leon Hammond. But unpredictability was the name of the game where Leon was concerned.

PRECIOUS INHERITANCE
Joan Moules

Karen's new life working for an authoress took her from Sussex to a foreign airstrip and a kidnapping; to a real life adventure as gripping as any in the books she typed.

VISION OF LOVE
Grace Richmond

When Kathy takes over the rundown country kennels she finds Alec Stinton, a local vet, very helpful. But their friendship arouses bitter jealousy and a tragedy seems inevitable.

CRUSADING NURSE
Jane Converse

It was handsome Dr. Corbett who opened Nurse Susan Leighton's eyes and who set her off on a lonely crusade against some powerful enemies and a shattering struggle against the man she loved.

WILD ENCHANTMENT
Christina Green

Rowan's agreeable new boss had a dream of creating a famous perfume using her precious Silverstar, but Rowan's plans were very different.

DESERT ROMANCE
Irene Ord

Sally agrees to take her sister Pam's place as La Chartreuse the dancer, but she finds out there is more to it than dyeing her hair red and looking like her sister.

HEART OF ICE
Marie Sidney

How was January to know that not only would the warmth of the Swiss people thaw out her frozen heart, but that she too would play her part in helping someone to live again?

LUCKY IN LOVE
Margaret Wood

Companion-secretary to wealthy gambler Laura Duxford, who lived in Monaco, seemed to Melanie a fabulous job. Especially as Melanie had already lost her heart to Laura's son, Julian.

NURSE TO PRINCESS JASMINE
Lilian Woodward

Nick's surgeon brother, Tom, performs an operation on an Arabian princess, and she invites Tom, Nick and his fiancé to Omander, where a web of deceit and intrigue closes about them.

THE WAYWARD HEART
Eileen Barry

Disaster-prone Katherine's nickname was "Kate Calamity", but her boss went too far with an outrageous proposal, which because of her latest disaster, she could not refuse.

FOUR WEEKS IN WINTER
Jane Donnelly

Tessa wasn't looking forward to meeting Paul Mellor again — she had made a fool of herself over him once before. But was Orme Jared's solution to her problem likely to be the right one?

SURGERY BY THE SEA
Sheila Douglas

Medical student Meg hadn't really wanted to go and work with a G.P. on the Welsh coast although the job had its compensations. But Owen Roberts was certainly not one of them!

HEAVEN IS HIGH
Anne Hampson

The new heir to the Manor of Marbeck had been found. But it was rather unfortunate that when he arrived unexpectedly he found an uninvited guest, complete with stetson and high boots.

LOVE WILL COME
Sarah Devon

June Baker's boss was not really her idea of her ideal man, but when she went from third typist to boss's secretary overnight she began to change her mind.

ESCAPE TO ROMANCE
Kay Winchester

Oliver and Jean first met on Swale Island. They were both trying to begin their lives afresh, but neither had bargained for complications from the past.

CASTLE IN THE SUN
Cora Mayne

Emma's invalid sister, Kym, needed a warm climate, and Emma jumped at the chance of a job on a Mediterranean island. But Emma soon finds that intrigues and hazards lurk on the sunlit isle.

BEWARE OF LOVE
Kay Winchester

Carol Brampton resumes her nursing career when her family is killed in a car accident. With Dr. Patrick Farrell she begins to pick up the pieces of her life, but is bitterly hurt when insinuations are made about her to Patrick.

DARLING REBEL
Sarah Devon

When Jason Farradale's secretary met with an accident, her glamorous stand-in was quite unable to deal with one problem in particular.

THE PRICE OF PARADISE
Jane Arbor

It was a shock to Fern to meet her estranged husband on an island in the middle of the Indian Ocean, but to discover that her father had engineered it puzzled Fern. What did he hope to achieve?

DOCTOR IN PLASTER
Lisa Cooper

When Dr. Scott Sutcliffe is injured, Nurse Caroline Hurst has to cope with a very demanding private case. But when she realises her exasperating patient has stolen her heart, how can Caroline possibly stay?

A TOUCH OF HONEY
Lucy Gillen

Before she took the job as secretary to author Robert Dean, Cadie had heard how charming he was, but that wasn't her first impression at all.

№		№		№		№	
1	NOV 2008			49	12/09	73	
2	4/14	26		50	4/19	74	
3		27		51		75	
4		28		52		76	
5		29		53		77	4/10
6	8/63	30	5/13	54		78	
7	10/07	31		55		79	
8	6/06	32		56		80	
9		33		57		81	
10		34		58		82	
11		35		59		83	
12	1/13	36		60		84	
13		37	11/16	61		85	
14	8/15	38		62		86	
15	8/12	39	12/17	63		87	
16		40		64		88	
17		41		65		89	
18		42		66		90	
19		43		67		91	
20	12/13	44		68		92	
21		45	8/17	69		COMMUNITY	
22		46	2/15	70		SERVICES	
23		47		71		NPT/111	
24		48		72			

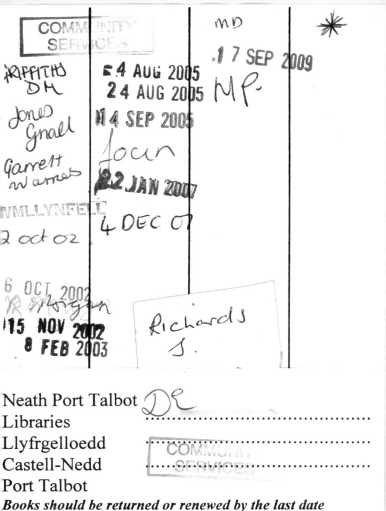